I'VE A FEELING
WE'RE NOT IN
KANSAS ANYMORE

I've a Feeling We're Not in Kansas Anymore:

Tales from Gay Manhattan

ETHAN MORDDEN

St. Martin's Press   New York

Some of these stories have appeared in somewhat different form in *Christopher Street* magazine.

Design by Laura Hough

Library of Congress Cataloging in Publication Data

Mordden, Ethan
  I've a feeling we're not in Kansas anymore.

  I. Title.
PS3563.O771719   1985   813'.54   85–10898
ISBN 0-312-40291-0

First Edition

10 9 8 7 6 5 4 3 2 1

To Michael Denneny,
sine qua non

Contents

Acknowledgments

The author wishes to acknowledge the strategic collaboration of the house team, which, he is glad to note, still includes the masterful Ina Shapiro, one of the most precise of stylists. Paul Liepa keeps a yare ship, Deborah Daly is indispensable in jacket-art meetings, Izume Inoue presents a unique rendering of The Emerald City of Manhattan on the cover, Laura Hough designed what IBM would call a "reader-friendly" book, Carol Shookhoff assisted in the typing of a printer-friendly manuscript, and, for the home side, there remains the redoubtable Dorothy Pittman, the author's best friend and agent, in that order. As for Michael Denneny, the editor of this book, I have expressed my feelings a few pages to the fore.

In particular, I would like to thank Charles Ortleb, the founder and publisher of *Christopher Street*, where a substantial share of post-Stonewall gay lit has originated—not because writers have battered their way in, but because Chuck personally stimulated, encouraged, and in some cases helped subsidize their careers. Without his insistence that gays maintain at least one forum for new journalists, storytellers, and poets, gay publishing might have consisted of nothing but an occasional shuddering of the linotype's chromosomes.

Preface

I have sat with friends—and I mean very close friends—on those long nights at the Pines, listening to the ocean dancing about our mysterious island, and on those long days at the brunch table, trying to remember to be urbane, and on those odd, ironic afternoons of confessing feelings of such intimate enthusiasm or disappointment that one regrets having made them for the rest of one's life. We have traded tales, my buddies and I: of affairs, encounters, discoveries, weekends, parties, secrets, fears, self-promotions—of fantasies that we make real in the telling.

Well, it occurs to me that all of gay life is stories—that all these stories are about love somehow or other, and that many jests are made in them, though the overall feeling may be sad. One's life breaks into episodes, chapters of a picaresque adventure. As each episode ends, the material for the next shifts into place. Defunct characters cede to new ones, though a few figures—the best friends—hold their places throughout. A happy ending must be temporary, and a gloomy one may yield to surprising amusement without warning. It is a lively life I sing, with but two constants: humor and friendship. I am looking back now on what I have seen and heard, and on the men I have known, and on certain perceptions I am reluctantly compelled to share. And these are my tales . . .

I'VE A FEELING
WE'RE NOT IN
KANSAS ANYMORE

Interview with
the Drag Queen

At night, writing longhand in a spiral notebook at my desk, I can see my reflection in a window washed in lamplight, as if I were working before a mirror. I have a romance going that I am my characters, and can put on any of their faces at will. I can be all forearm and fist, or startled behind spectacles; I can wear my college sweatshirt, or hold my pen in an old-fashioned manner. When I view my reflection in the window, I am telling stories.

I say this because I recall that the drag queen recounted her saga into a great mirror that stood just over my left shoulder. She scarcely looked at me, or at her friend Paul, who had brought me to her.

"You must tell her story," Paul had urged. "This is gay history."

No, I was writing nonfiction then. I had no reflection. "I wouldn't know where to sell it," I told him. No stories.

"Try," he said. "Just take it down. *Someday.*"

I was intrigued. Paul arranged it, took me to a shabby walkup where Bleecker Street meets The Bowery, introduced us, and—breaking his word of honor not to leave me alone—walked out. "You'll see," he murmured. "See what?" I answered; he was already at the door, waving.

"'Who was that masked man?'" I quoted, to cover my embarrassment. And: "Why does everyone I know run out on me after five minutes?"

This was eleven years ago. The drag queen was perhaps

1

fifty. Black cocktail dress, spike heels, cabaret mascara, and opera jewelry.

"When Miss Titania gave an order, you obeyed or that's it, you were out! You were glue. You were *grovel!* I mean. Miss Titania was the very certain queen of the Heat Rack—and was she big, I ask you? Bigger than a Zulu's dingus on Thursday night. Big in *spirit!* Miss Titania had her court, and everyone else was dogmeat when Miss Titania got through. Ask anyone. I don't know where they are now, but you ask them."

My pen flew. "Where's Miss Titania now?" I asked.

The drag queen shrugged. "It's all gone, so that is no question at all to me. Now every man in the city looks like trade in those muscle shirts, with those demure little bags like they're carrying their makeup kit or I don't know what. I don't think there's a man in New York who isn't available. Once even the gays were straight; now all the straights are gay. New York doesn't like queens anymore, regardless. We're the old revolutionaries. They say we dressed up because we were flops as men. Born to be freaks. They say we didn't care what other folks thought." She lit a cigarette like a woman, blowing the match out; and held it like a man, between thumb and forefinger. "Well, it's not true. We dressed up so they could see how lovely we are. We hope they see it."

"What if they don't?"

"Then we say something pungent."

"Tell me about Miss Titania."

"She was ruthless. The Heat Rack was her court, and *no one* upstaged her. The dire episodes! Once an upstart southern belle came in out of nowhere—I suspect Scranton—and there she was, taking up space and flouting Miss Titania. I will never forget—'Mr. Sandman' was playing on the juke, and Miss Titania liked to sing along, you know, such as 'Mr. Sandman, please make me cream.' A slightly altered version of the original, as I recall. Well, La Southern Comfort cries out, 'Deyah me, it would surely take the entiyah football teyum? at Ole Miss? to make you-all creayum, I'm shuah?' And there

2

was such silence in the whole place. Except for 'Mr. Sandman.' I *mean*. Even the toughest trade shut up. And Miss Titania. She looks at that no-good, lightweight daredevil, and smiles her famous smile and puts down her drink and fan. And suddenly, I don't know, it couldn't have been more than a few seconds, but Miss Titania flies across the room and rips the hair right off that southern girl's head—I mean her wig, truly; did you think I meant her skull hair? because, really, what an odd look you're wearing—and then Miss Titania rends the bodice of the southern girl's gown and pulls off her pathetic training bra or whatever she had on, and we are all roaring with laughter, so that southern girl runs into the ladies' and won't come out till the place is closed. We never saw her after that. Because you *don't* challenge the queen in her own court.

"And Miss Titania was the absolute queen. Even the Duchess of Diva, who presided over Carney's on Thirty-eighth Street—even she knew better than to tangle with Miss Titania. And the Duchess was a gigantic mother. She must have weighed three hundred pounds. Always wore black, for her husband. He died in the war. And did she have a savage streak. Everyone feared her. But Miss Titania had the prestige."

"Tell me more about the Heat Rack."

"Or the Pleasure Bar, or Folly's, or The Demitasse, or Club La Bohème, or sometimes no name at all. It changed by the week. To me it was always the Heat Rack, because that's what they called it when I made my choice."

"Your choice?"

"Between love and beauty. Surely you know that every queen must choose between living for the one or the other. You can't have both." She rose and presented herself to the mirror pensively. "I chose beauty, because I imagined that those who know about love can never have it. Do you think so, too?"

I was young then, and never thought about it. Now, in my window, I wonder. The woman across the way, in direct line of my desk, becomes unnerved at my concentration, and lowers her blinds.

"The bars today are just saloons," the drag queen goes on. "The Heat Rack was our fortress and fraternity, the only place where *we* made the rules. We rated the beauty and arranged the love stories." She sweeps through the dismal room, touching things. "The whole world is just queens, johns, trade, and cops. The whole world. And Miss Titania kept them *all* in line. Yes. Yes. Yes. And she was kind and beautiful."

She is not speaking to me.

"The johns you respect. The trade you screw. The cops you ignore. Life is so simple in the Heat Rack. Now I'll tell you the difference between queens and trade."

She is looking hard at me for the first time.

"Queens are afraid that every horrible insult hurled at them is true. Trade is impervious to insult."

I take notes.

"That's why these Stonewall men all look like cowboys. They think if they play trade they won't have their feelings hurt. I would imagine that is why you've got dark glasses on right now."

"I always have dark glasses on."

"That's fascinating, no doubt. But how nice of you to wear a tie for me, all the same. The johns always wore ties."

In my window, it's always T-shirts. Once I came home from the opera so keen to write I sat down in my suit. Then I looked up and thought, "Who is that man?"

"The johns were so nice. All those years at the Heat Rack, never did I have to buy my own drink. Of course, they were living for love, so they were always getting wounded."

"What does trade live for?"

"To torment queens. That's why Miss Titania had to enforce the regulations so strictly, to keep trade from cheating the johns and breaking their hearts. Or making a ruckus, which they always did. Or showing off their stupid tattoos with a lady present. And some of them never washed and you

4

could smell their asses all the way across the room. Now, the Duchess of Diva, she let trade run *rampant* in her court. Mind you, I'm for a free market. But you give trade their liberty and what do you have?"

"Tell me."

"A world in which beauty passes the laws and all lovers go mad. I'm sure you know this, a writer. Do you write poems?"

"Never."

"I yearn for poetry. But no one rhymes anymore. No one lives for beauty. Everything is . . . *meaning*. There's always a message now. What's the good in a message when a pretty picture tells you everything you need to know?

"Now, I can tell you, on some nights the Heat Rack was the prettiest picture you ever hoped to see. In summer, let me say. The johns in the dark corners or sitting in the back booths, out of the way. And trade all around, some shirtless and so still, not looking to see who saw them. Three or four, perhaps, loafing at the pool table—not even playing, I expect, just filling out the tableau, making silly jokes and rubbing each other's necks and getting pensive. And the queens were near, doting. You would look for a moment at all this, all around, and it was like a painting. It was magic, regardless.

"But you can dote too much. And trade will take control if they can. That's why Miss Titania . . . once . . . I shouldn't tell you this, I suppose. You Stonewall boys don't understand the patterns of love discipline. What do you live for, you cowboys? What stirs you? Does the sight of a trade's crack, all trembling and open to assault . . . does it stir you? Do you want me to stop?"

"Go on."

"Well, once Miss Titania determined that a certain trade would have to be disciplined. A beautiful galoot, big and dark, the cruel kind. Like your father or some such. *Tales of the Woodshed?* Big, breezy galoots, so lazy and mean. This one was called Carl, and he was swindling the johns. He'd go with them but wouldn't let them do anything. Then he'd flex his huge muscles and say they'd better give him a tip, and he'd empty their wallets. He even pulled this on the queens! I mean, in Miss Titania's court, you *never* smooth a queen! Well. So Miss Titania and the Duchess of Diva made a date at Miss Titania's place with this trade, Carl. Funny name for trade. They're usually Blue or Tex or so what. Miss Titania and the Duchess, they knock Carl out with a mickey . . . do they still call them mickeys?"

"Oddly enough, that's exactly the word a friend of mine used recently when some guy got into his apartment and—"

"Who's being interviewed, anyway?" she cried, all chin and cheekbones.

"Carry on."

"It was a *rhetorical* question. So Miss Titania and the Duchess strip Carl and tie him to the bed on his stomach, and they call the court over to watch, because you have to humiliate trade to reform them. And I thoroughly approve of this, because they can become almost sweet after they've had their asses whipped. The Duchess of Diva—whose sense of tact, I must tell you, runs way to the left of disreputable—wanted to tie Carl down face up, so she could whip his chest and cock and even his face. She would have, too. But Miss Titania knows what's right. Except as she was getting ready to whip that boy's ass, Miss Titania begins to realize what a beautiful thing it is to tenderize a man like that. Sweeten him up. Make him so sweet. It's a dreamy thing. Meanwhile, Carl is coming to and the Duchess is telling him off but good about how he'd better not try his tricks in *her* court, which is very funny because he's so groggy he doesn't know what *planet* he's on. And Miss Titania is just gazing upon him. How his shoulder skin ripples as he's struggling against the rope and how his ass quivers as she lays the whip so gently upon it. And then Carl is bellowing like a bull, how he'll kill us all. But Miss Titania knows that a beautiful stud was born to be whipped, and to see him stretched out nude and helpless is the most beautiful thing in the world. And his ass is so lovely as she parts it to inhale the stink of him . . ."

6

I would rehearse dialogue in my window, but how does one look saying this? Because truth is not beauty. Is *not*.

"... and she knows that he must be whipped, and how good that would be, and of course the Duchess is shrieking, 'Let's rip him up!' all over the room. She has *no* sense of timing. But Miss Titania spreads Carl's legs wider and wider as she strokes his thighs. She must calm him down, it's true. And then he's quiet. He knows he must be sweetened, and that is the secret that queens and trade share. You couldn't hear a sound in the place as Miss Titania soothed Carl's hole with her tongue and slowly worked it open, and Carl's groaning like a wild beast who doesn't care what anyone knows about him. I truly believe that that is the most beautiful sound in the world. Don't you?"

"No."

She looks at me now, quite frankly. "To be sure. And what do you call the most beautiful sound?"

"*La Mer?*"

The drag queen looks away as if she would never look back again. "Who's she?"

"It's music."

"Miss Titania rimmed and rimmed," the drag queen insisted. "It was the most spectacular rim job since Scheherazade. Even the Duchess of Diva held her peace as she looked on, and there wasn't a soul in that room who wouldn't have given a year of life to be in Miss Titania's place. Carl's head was swaying on his neck like a broken toy, and he kept saying, 'No. No. No. No.' I wonder why he said that. He was crying. A big, dashing, empty fuck-monster like that, crying. Can you imagine? And when it was done and Carl had been rimmed inside and out, the Duchess of Diva untied him and all the court looked upon him. He had not been whipped, yet he was sweetened. As if he had been cleaned out in his *mind*. He would give no trouble from now on, because everyone had watched. They saw him, do you see? But Miss Titania saw nothing. She was swaying in mid-air as if in a trance. I believe she was in a state of grace, truly. And Carl went into the bathroom and he wouldn't come out."

"Just like that southern queen who offended Miss—"

She flared up like a lighter. "How dare you? It's not the same at all!"

"Well, in outline—"

"*Trade is not like queens!* Now, do you understand? And they *never* will be!"

"Which would you rather be, if you could choose and start all over?"

She is quiet. "I lived for beauty. That was my choice." I take notes.

"You don't think that is sufficient, you Stonewall cowboy. Do you? I suppose you live for music. How grand."

"Music is a form of beauty, isn't it?"

"No. Beauty is not music. Beauty is a pretty picture. I told you that. Oh, no—no, I'll give you something for your piece. Yes. Someone asked Miss Titania once, 'What is beauty?' You know what she said? And I quote: 'Beauty is the death of the drag queen.' *There!*"

She sighed as I wrote. Eleven years ago there was no place to print such tales as this. "Just take it down," Paul had said, and he added, "You'll see."

She lit another cigarette. "It's true. We had to die so you cowboys could live. Not that we wanted to. No one asked us, regardless. But people who believe every horrible insult are of no use to anyone now. That is not part of survival. No. This society believes in trade. Even if all the trade is imitation. Cops and johns, that's all that's left. That's all that's real. The need and the threat. Where's beauty now, penscratcher?"

I looked up from my notebook. I looked at her and she looked back. She smiled.

"You think we have no feelings," she said. "Is that it?" I waited.

"Feelings, dressed like this? Feelings? In a place called the Heat Rack? The Demitasse? Feelings, that I am thrilled by the simple sight of a tie? I don't have feelings, right? Yes?

8

Yes?" She screamed in that dreary room; I hear it yet. *"Say yes!"*

And I said, "Yes." Because that is the impression they infix.

She calmed down quite suddenly. "Yes," she said. "Yes, thank you." She nodded. "How right you are. We don't have feelings. We learn to live without them."

That sounded like the end of the last stanza. I rose to go.

"Where will your piece be printed," she asked, "and when? I must order copies for all the gang."

"You still see them, then?"

"Alas." She raised her hand, palm to me. "Not for a terribly long time. But wouldn't it be dramatic to track them down for the occasion?"

"Do you think you could find Miss Titania?"

"No one will ever find Miss Titania. She was the first to die, you see. Now, tell me—*The New York Times? McCall's?* Would they want a picture, dare I hope?"

"Let's wing it," I said, while visualizing the editors of the *Times* coming upon that line about the Zulu's dingus. And *McCall's!*

"What did you think?" Paul asked me on the phone a bit later.

"I think Miss Titania is the one I should have interviewed. There the story lies."

"You jerk," he said. "That *is* Miss Titania."

That *was* Miss Titania, my window tells me, eleven years later; it took that long for me to believe my ears. My eyes I trust by the moment, but who is that masked man? Who tells me these terrible tales? I wish I could choose between beauty and love; I wish life were so trim; I, too, like a pretty picture. But I think the meaning matters more. Staring straight into my window to the disgust of my neighbor, I am bewildered, saddened, offended, and amazed. God make me as honest a storyteller as the drag queen was.

The Straight;
or, Field Expedients

When my windows are not reflecting the local countenance, they give out on a great hole from which an office tower has been rising, somewhat feyly (I think) referred to on the hoarding as "Third Avenue at Fifty-third Street."

So be it. But in the early 1970s, it was all brownstones—especially one, a great box of stories that I would gaze upon from my desk. There was the ancient couple, top left, who never washed their windows. There were the Spanish-speaking queens, middle right, with the yapping chihuahua and the live-in Puerto Rican who watered the hanging garden on the fire escape in the nude. There were the bohemians next to them—he played cello and she painted—and my friend Alex just above. Next to him was a plain straight couple; the woman was seldom seen, the man always around.

As I wrote, typed, and fretted at the dictionary, I would spot this man in his window, looking, sitting, guzzling beer, waiting. He had very long hair, which he sometimes wore in a ponytail, heavy arms and thighs, and (apparently) no clothing but boxer shorts. Gay, he would have gymmed himself inside of a year into a gleaming demon. But straights often like themselves as they are; it's an arcane grade of hot I've never understood.

My friend Alex would regale me with tales of this couple. One season, the woman was cute and the man a nerd. Next season, she was standoffish and he vaguely sweet. They fought, they cooed, they bought a stereo, she made perfect strudel, he got a job. . . .

"Why tell me these stories?" I finally asked. "All straight stories are the same. What's in it for us?"

Even when they broke up, the tale lacked interest. But my best friend Dennis Savage was thrilled. "Nowadays," he said, "when a straight couple busts up, the man always turns gay. Or the woman. You never know with straights."

"This woman isn't gay," said Alex. "Karen. She left him because he wasn't smart enough for her."

"He was smart enough to keep the apartment."

"She went to California. *That's* smart."

"Anyway, I've seen this guy but plenty," I told Dennis Savage. "Nothing."

"How can you tell this far off?" Alex countered. "Besides, you've never met him. He happens to be—" Noting that we were watching him like trolls observing a Billy Goat Gruff crossing our bridge, he stopped. "He's a nice man. Joe Dolan."

Dennis Savage went into a barfing pantomime as I held my nose.

"That," I said, "is the straightest name I ever heard."

"What's a gay name?" asked Alex.

"Dorinda Spreddem," I offered. "Nosy Porker."

"Maytag de Washer," Dennis Savage suggested. "Rosemary de Tramp."

"Humungous Layman."

"Will you stop?" Alex pleaded. "Will you, please?"

"Don't get serious about him," Dennis Savage advised. "Those crushes on the straight next door are destructive. Because straight is straight and they never cross that line, no matter how drunk they get, no matter how mad they get at women, no matter—"

"We've already had sex," Alex said. "All the way, everything. Several times."

The room was so quiet we could hear the appliances depreciating. Alex got up and looked out the window at his building for a long while. "He's there now, watching a baseball game or somesuch. And when it's over he'll knock on my door. He says I'm good to talk to."

"So he is gay after all," said Dennis Savage.

"He lived with Karen for two years. They were lovers."

"An act."

"I was there! I saw them together! You can fool your parents and your co-workers, but not your gay neighbor. It's no act."

"You're saying that this man came on to you several times and he's not gay?"

"I'm saying that everything about him is straight. Including the way he comes on."

Dennis Savage sighed. "Now I'm fascinated. Tell."

"I certainly will not!"

"Oh, let me guess. He came over one night and asked if you know how to give a backrub."

"No, it wasn't—"

"He was in red velvet, a stole, and a cloche hat, and you said—"

"How can you make fun of something so *intime* and dear, and so terribly secret?"

"Will you hark at him?" Dennis Savage exclaimed to me. "*Intime!*"

"All right!" Alex paced, stopped, and paced again. "All right, I'll tell. Just don't jeer any more. Don't mock things you don't understand."

"Listen, Alex," said Dennis Savage, "I was setting Stonewall style when you were running around in a propeller beanie, so don't tell me what I understand or don't." He turned to me. "Do I know gay or don't I?"

"I'll say," I agreed. "You've gone down on everything but the Lusitania."

"Look!" cried Alex. "Do you want the story or not?"

It was a familiar one: boy loses girl, boy turns to local ear for sympathy, and a friendship is born. "He'd visit every night, or I'd go to his place. Dropping in, you know? We just talked. For hours, sometimes. He'd be going on about 'ladies' all the time. This lady in Dallas, this lady in Chicago, do I have a lady, how do I address a lady. And I just wanted him to scoop me up . . ." He gazed out my window. "Not once did he look at me ambiguously. He never laid a hand on me. I could have been his uncle.

"Then one night, while we were watching some football or basketball game on television, he started to tell me how ladies never really liked him. How they'd put up with him when they were between true loves. *Put up with him*—that was how he said it. Even Karen, after all that time . . . even she thought he was a goon. A goon, he said. Because he didn't . . . he wasn't . . . smooth enough or something. Well, one woman's goon is another . . . man's . . . if you see what I mean. And he was telling me about the different ways of turning ladies on. Some men have a tattoo in a fancy place. You know? And they show it. Or some have subtle speeches worked out. And one friend of his, he said, used to show his ladies photographs of himself kissing another man. And he . . . asked me what I thought of that. I was thinking that if all the women he liked thought he was a goon, maybe he should . . . maybe take some photographs himself. Because he isn't handsome, I know, but he's . . . strong. He's nice to me." Alex cleared his throat. "He only wants to be liked, you know? He'll do anything to be liked. And I saw that. And I . . . well . . ."

"You liked him," I put in. "That's what it is."

"Well, I told him maybe he should try making such photographs. And he laughed and said, 'Would you make them with me?' I guessed he was joking. But he kept talking about it. He told me Karen doesn't really know him. And how I'm so much nicer to him. And how . . . how we should make those pictures. And . . . out of nowhere . . . he said, 'I sure would like to ream you.' Just like that. I was so startled I couldn't speak. I thought I'd misheard him. But he went on. 'I won't hurt you,' he said. 'I just want to put my cock in you and see what you're like. We can be buddies, okay?'" He turned back to us. "Come and see. He's standing in the window."

We got there so fast we almost crashed through the glass. There he was, looking at us. Alex smiled and waved, and Joe wiggled his index finger at him in that "Come here" gesture that kids use.

"So you're buddies," Dennis Savage said as Alex got his coat on.

"One catch," Alex replied. "We can't call it by name. It's okay only if you don't admit you're doing it. The day I say 'gay' he'll drop me."

"Or kill you."

"He wouldn't hurt me. He only gets mad at strangers."

I don't know whether Alex thought of Dennis Savage and me as the natural strangers of Joe Dolan, but he kept the man to himself. Perhaps he thought exposure to outright gays might threaten their touchy diplomacy. A lover who won't bear the word *gay* obviously won't be comfortable around practitioners of the style.

So we all left it thus. From my desk, spotting Joe watching at his window, I gave him no more than a glance. And the days stole by me; and I wrote; and it was with some shock that I noticed one time that Joe the Straight had cut his hair and grown a clone moustache. Alex tried to shrug it away when I ran into him in Sloan's. "I don't know," he said. "He just . . . he decided . . ." He faked an elaborate pantomime with the tuna cans, apparently dismissing me.

"I'm not moving," I told him.

He wouldn't look up. "He joined a gym, too. He's really gotten into it. He's quite . . . different . . ."

"Are you disappointed? Or Columbus sighting America?"

He grew fierce. "I wish you'd stop."

"I'm too curious to stop. Is he gay or isn't he?"

"Is it always war or peace? Comic or tragic?"

"If you're fighting, it's war; if you're not, it's peace. If it's about courtship, it's comic; if it's about honor, it's tragic. And if it makes love to men, it's gay."

14

He stared at me for a spell, said, "I can remember when I thought you might be my best friend," and walked out.

What had got into me? It's none of my business whether Alex plays comedy or tragedy. Two days later he called, apologized, and invited me to dinner.

So I officially met Joe, who couldn't have looked gayer in his white T-shirt, Levi's, and Frye boots. He didn't *seem* gay, lacking both self-willing sensuality and self-spoofing satire. But he also lacked the self-righteous coarseness of proletarian straight culture. He was placeless, a man without a side in the war. He seemed unaware of Alex unless directly addressing him, yet I felt a marvelous tension in the averting of their eyes. While we were clearing the table, I caught him watching Alex, who was at the sink. Joe picked up a glass, took it to Alex, pressed it into his grasp, and gently rubbed his fingers. "Yeah," he said. Then he put his hand on Alex's neck and traced a finger along his eyebrows, shifting weight from foot to foot as if dancing. "Oh yeah," he went on, nabbing Alex's eyes with his own, and he purred a little, then concluded, "Oh, that's real nice." It was the most pornographic act I'd ever witnessed.

"Well?" Dennis Savage asked later. "Is he or isn't he? And if you don't tell me, I'll make you rim the Roach Motel."

"Let me point out that there is an incredibly vicious dish-queen in this room and it isn't me. Can I tell who it is?"

"Can we please stop with this and tell me if Joe Dolan is gay!"

"I don't know what he is. He doesn't seem straight and he doesn't seem gay."

"Is he still a big dull lump? Sexually?"

"Well . . . no."

"You mean he's hot?"

"It depends on . . . actually—"

Dennis Savage closed in. "You wake up and he's in your bed. Either you say, 'Get out of this bed' or you say 'Help me

15

make it through the night.' Which? Pick one only." I just looked at him. "He's hot, isn't he? He has the look, doesn't he? He knows how to do it, right? *Right?*"

"Maybe."

"I hope you never join the CIA. Because if we're West Berlin, and the KGB is East Berlin, where would you be? *Middle* Berlin, right?"

"This is where I paint a telephone on your face and dial you with ice-cube tongs."

"Does he have feelings?"

That halted me. "Who doesn't?"

"Most straights don't. Or no one knows for sure. Only a straight could tell us, and no straight is sensitive enough to know what feelings are."

"Are you saying that straights are androids?"

"No, I'm saying that straights are video games."

"You know," I said, "it's just possible that he is straight. That, in fact, he took Alex to bed because after a lifetime of failing to get women to regard him as anything but an ork, he decided to go with someone who admired him. Or . . . I don't know. Maybe he's just another nerd exploding out of his closet."

"Does he, I repeat, have feelings?"

"Did gays have feelings in the 1940s, when no one tolerated their feelings? Joe Dolan may simply be an uninformed homosexual."

"That's gay."

"Stop playing king of the Circuit and look at it from someone else's point of view, all right? He comes from some small town where everything is *Father Knows Best*. He has no access to all the media snitching. He never reads a book, much less hangs out at the opera or blunders into a gay bar. He could miss the whole thing. And he grows up thinking he'd better hide his sexuality, because he thinks he's the only one—or, who knows?, maybe everyone hides it. But it's hard to be selective in such matters, so he hides *everything*. Including his feelings. That, my friend, is what gay life was like in

16

the old days. One man befriends another, opportunity strikes, they become buddies. And only the other buddies know what they are. Do you like that story?"

"He's hot, isn't he?"

"Yes, he's hot."

"Not handsome or charming."

"No."

"Not even fun."

"Not yet."

"But strong and loyal. Am I correct?"

"You are smug, but correct."

"When will he reveal his feelings?"

"When Alex hurts him, and he weeps in despair."

Dennis Savage exhaled with contentment and went into the kitchen to refill the glasses. "I didn't care for this adventure before, but now I love it. Except you're wrong about one piece. Alex will not hurt Joe Dolan. He's been left out of too much to blow something this good."

"You don't know Alex."

Dennis Savage handed me wine. "Did he hurt you?"

I raised my glass. "To new friends," I said.

Our new friend was Joe, because Alex was now bringing him out. Joe still thought of movies as something you see rather than discuss, had no use for cabaret, and didn't know how to dance: there was nothing to bring. But his months at the gym had styled him smartly, and he could pass. He had lost his nondescript straight's fleshiness; he was cut and basted. His pants were tight, his hands heavy, his nipples offensive. At the Tenth Floor one night, Dennis Savage and I overheard two kids discussing some avatar when suddenly we realized that they were referring to Joe, dancing shirtless with Alex. We watched the crowd watching them, knew that Joe was crossing over, wondered how it felt to him, took in the music and the crowd and the hunger, and joined Joe and Alex on the floor.

It was a gala last night before the summer break, and the room was packed. How amazing to think back and realize that the scene that would eventually fill and jade The Saint had started out in that undecorated little den of innocence. It was hard to dance without jostling one's neighbors, yet someone behind Joe was taking up far too much room, throwing his arms around, clapping and posing. He was knocking into everyone around him, and finally Joe told him, in a neutral tone, "Look, would you mind keeping your hands to yourself?"

"Why don't you fuck your panties, you frump?" said the stranger, a high-voltage little queen with the voice of transvestite Brillo.

"Okay," said Joe, still evenly. "Now you can move out of our part of the floor, or you're going to wish you did."

"Says who, you bitch?" With that the stranger shoved Joe at the rest of us, a foolish act given their respective sizes. Joe hauled back and, with a hoarse cry, felled his foe.

"Oh shit!" the queen screamed, feeling blood at his nose, as his friends whimpered and giggled. "Oh, help me!"

"You asked for it," Joe told him.

Alex was furious. "Did you have to fight?" he whispered through his teeth. "What is this, a circus? A SWAT encounter?" He stormed off the floor. The rest of us followed, while Joe's opponent, his coterie, and thrilled bystanders played out The Theatre of the Punched-Out Queen.

Had we been smart, we would have called it a night. But no, we went on to Dennis Savage's place, with Alex seething and Joe bewildered. I knew there was more to come, and, yes, no sooner did our host pour out the wine than Joe gave Alex his opening by rehearsing the episode.

"He shoved me, didn't he?" he asked. "What was I supposed to do, thank him?"

"You don't fight," Alex spit at him, "at the Tenth Floor."

"It's not my fault where it happened."

"*Your* behavior is *your* fault!"

Joe turned away, struggling to control his anger.

"How about some music?" I asked. "Some Nino Rota?"

"*Otto e Mezzo!*" cried Dennis Savage.

"*Giulietta degli Spiriti!*"

Alex viewed us as if we were the Barry Sisters making a comeback singing "Que Sera, Sera" in his bathroom, and returned to Joe.

"You're like something just off the bus from Akron. You're not ready for the social life. You're a pushy clod."

"I never said I wasn't. And why do we have to go dancing? Or out to dinner with your ooh-la-la friends?" He turned to us. "I don't mean you two." We felt like the Barry Sisters, barred from presenting an Academy Award backstage at the last minute on account of deficient ooh-la-la. "But some of your friends treat me as if—"

"And they're *right!*"

"I don't want to go to these places. Why can't we just be together? That's all I want." He went to Alex, held him by the waist, and saw him so acutely all three of us were transfixed. Looked and *saw.* "Just to be with you. To pump you and cream you."

"You beggar!" Alex shouted. "You *filth!* You dare say this in front of them?"

We seemed to be the Barry Sisters, stumbling onstage during a performance of *Private Lives.*

"Why shouldn't I? They know we're buddies."

"We're *not* buddies! *We are not!*" Dennis Savage had never seen Alex like this; I had. "We're *lovers.* We're men who fuck together. Your cock in my ass. Lovers, Joe. Say the word 'gay.' Say 'lovers'!"

"That's *enough!*"

"Gay is the word, Joe. That lovers use, you know? Gay means you're a beautiful muscle dude who rides me out of my mind. Tell them how your body moves. We're filth. We'll tell them together. Then you can sock me, too."

Joe grabbed Alex, to hold or to hurt him, but he kept changing his grip and finally he put his hand over Alex's mouth. "I know what we are," he said. "I know about love and things. I'm not a beast. I'm *not* a beast. I just don't want to be pushed around. That guy at the dancing was asking for it. He started it." He let go of Alex and faced us. "He says I'm filth and then he says I'm beautiful. What am I supposed to think?"

"You're supposed to think you're gay," Alex told him. "Say it: say 'Joe Dolan is gay.' Say 'Joe Dolan is a beast.'"

Joe hesitated, shook his head, then tried to grab Alex again.

"A beast," Alex pursued, pushing Joe away. "How can you love men when you fight them? You have no smarts. You have no patience. You have no ambition. You have no sensitivity. You're a stupid hunk with thighs of death, that's all. And when I tire of you or you tire of me, you'll be nothing but Karen's castoff memory. How do you like it, beast? So you punched a pantywaist in a dance hall. Wow! Nice job, Thighs. Inside of three minutes, you can alienate everyone in a room. You've got the touch, Thighs!"

And Joe was weeping. "I did the right thing," he said. He wiped his eyes, but the tears kept coming. "How can you say that to me, Alex?"

"How beautiful," said Alex, "to see you cry."

"Would someone like a toasted bagel?" Dennis Savage asked.

"I'm not a beast," Joe insisted. "I'm your buddy."

"You're human garbage," Alex replied.

"Leave him alone, Alex," I said.

"He's a bully."

"He's had a good teacher."

"I did the right thing!" Joe grabbed Alex, spun him around, pushed him, held him, stroked his hair. Dennis Savage and I might have been the Barry Sisters screening *Psycho,* or perhaps *She Married Her Boss.* "Okay?" Joe went on. "Please! Okay?"

"Only if you call it by its name," said Alex. We could see his cock stirring at Joe's touch.

"Take me how I am."

"How you are," Alex persisted, "is a lewd queen."

20

"I'm a *man*."

"We're all lewd queens," Dennis Savage observed.

"Dennis Savage is a lewd queen," I explained. "I'm a man."

"Excuse me, but you're a princess."

"And you're the pea."

"Will you shut up?" Alex screamed. "How can we quarrel with you two playing fag vaudeville?"

"I love him," Joe told us. "I truly do. To hold him and talk with him and . . . the rest. Is that enough? I am saying that I love him."

"Make him say the word," said Alex.

"He cried before God and gays," Dennis Savage noted. "Justice is served." To me he added, "You were right—he wept."

"I don't know what anyone is talking about here," said Joe. He kept wiping his eyes and crying. "Do you think I'm a beast?" he asked me.

"That little queen started it and you finished it. As far as I go, you did the right thing."

We solemnly shook hands.

"Oh look!" Alex cried. "Look at the two *men!*"

"Now I think I *will* sock him!"

"No, Joe. Tell him to go fluff his puff."

"His . . . puff?"

"Just say it."

He gave me an odd look, but he said it: "Alex, go fluff your puff!"

Everyone was laughing. The fight was about courtship, not honor: a comedy.

"You call me horrible names and make fun of my morals," Joe told Alex. "You say you're glad that I cried. You call me a beast. And now we're all laughing. It's crazy! My face is wet with my own tears and I'm laughing!"

"Well, there you go, shweetheart," I said in my Humphrey Bogart voice. "Welcome to gay."

"That," said Dennis Savage, "is the *worst* Greta Garbo imitation I have ever heard."

The Mute Boy

Everyone has a smartest friend, a handsomest friend, a most famous friend, and a best friend. Mine are Lionel, Carlo, Eric, and Dennis Savage. Some of us have a sweetest friend, too; mine was Mac McNally. In a city where everyone you're supposed to want to meet turns out to be a ghoul, Mac was a hobbit: whimsical, sentimental, and tactfully frisky. He adored his friends; he was faultless and true. I wondered where he had got it from till the day one of his brothers showed up from the family seat near Racine. Over dinner, I saw Mac in an older, larger version—the same quick grin, the same eager nod of agreement, the same unselfish strength. I have seen (and had) my fill of brothers, but this one seemed to belong to some new genre in relationships, one of pledges made early, freely, and permanently. There were no delicacies of regret or disapproval in his affection for Mac, no fascism in his beautiful morals. He was that unheard-of thing in families, the relative who treats you as a perfect lover. Their intimacy was fearsome, like a ballet without music. I had heard it was a big tribe. "Are they all like that?" I asked later. Mac grinned and nodded.

By day Mac was a computer programmer—by night too, sometimes, depending on the project—but his great gift was writing, in the tightest, leanest style I've ever known. So, too, was Mac tight and lean, very light, very swift. But his eyes weighed a thousand pounds. Letters were his forte. I met him in the mail, in a note congratulating me on some book or other, forwarded by the publisher. I answer the nice ones, and so found myself in correspondence with an address just up the avenue, reading arresting disquisitions on a host of subjects, all of them love, in penciled block letters. One letter arrived with photographs, of Mac and four friends on summer holiday in Portugal, of Mac and an older couple camping in Maine, of Mac and his three brothers and their wives and children at the Thanksgiving bash.

"What is he, a tour guide?" asked Dennis Savage, when I showed him the pictures.

"You don't miss a chance to bring ants to the picnic, do you?"

"How come he's never alone? He's cute, anyway. When are you going to meet him?"

It comes down to that, doesn't it? The quest. It was Mac who broached the question, asking me to dinner—but it was a friend of his, Rolf something, who did the phoning.

"Mac's held up at work," he explained, "and we didn't know how late a day you keep." It sounded dotty to me, but I went along with it. On the afternoon of the date, Rolf called again. "Are we still on for tonight?" he asked.

"Of course."

"Fine. Just checking. We don't want Mac's feelings hurt in the slightest way, do we?"

"Did you hear I was going to hurt them?"

"No offense. But some New Yorkers are unreliable and I didn't want any misunderstanding."

"Have no fears. When it comes to appointments I'm sure as steel."

"That's what Mac's friends like to hear."

Maybe he is a tour guide, I thought as I hung up. I haven't had a call that strange since the last time I spoke to my mother.

Rolf opened the door. He was tall, handsome, and slightly gray, of the stalwart type that, I was to learn, marked Mac's cohort. My handshake is pretty solid, but his was a grip of grips: I felt like a glass of water meeting the North Sea. As

I came in, Rolf stood aside and there was Mac. He pointed at himself, pointed at me, touched his heart, and indicated the apartment with a sweep of his hand.

"I'm very pleased to meet you," said Rolf, "and my apartment is yours."

I looked at Rolf. Rolf looked dead on at Mac.

Mac and I shook hands and he picked up a glass, looking enquiringly at me. "What would you like to drink?" said Rolf.

I asked for wine.

Mac made a "fork in the road" with his index fingers, then upturned the palms in a questioning gesture.

"White or red?" said Rolf.

An incorrigible lush, I answered, "Whichever you have more of," making my lip movements as clear as possible. I must have looked like someone in an early Hollywood talkie, overtly proclaiming the new miracle of dialogue. Smiling, Mac slashed the air with a finger, put it to my lips, jabbed himself with his thumb, and, slowly drawing his open hands up to his ears, nodded once. "Speak normally," said Rolf, who was beginning to sound like a Conehead. "I can hear."

Mac poured wine for us. We sat. "I have to tell you," I began, "you write wonderful letters. I'm amazed at how many ideas you cram onto a single page."

Mac shook his head vigorously, pointed at me, deftly suggested writing as he pulled the finger back to stab his heart, made a circle with thumb and forefinger as his eyes appeared to read, raised the circle high in the air, and read more. "No," said Rolf, "your letters are the wonderful ones. They move me so I must reread them."

"I got it," I murmured, staring at Mac. Rolf was no longer the translation, but an echo. Mac's sign language was as eloquent as his letters were: his hands gave the message, their speed or angle lent nuance, and his face showed how the message and nuances felt. All you had to do was look. By the time the food appeared, I myself was performing Mac's "sounding"—his term, a correction of my faux pas, that delightful and exhausting night, in verbalizing the notion that I

24

was "speaking" for him. Fiercely shaking his head, he reached for one of the little pads lying all about the apartment, and with mischievous grace wrote me in those block letters I knew from the mail: "I do speak—without noise."

He was not deaf, only mute, apparently the reverse of the usual condition; even a fluke, for all I could guess, for I never asked. He was proud of his ability to cope with his impairment but, if not ashamed of it, reticent about it. His many friends protected him—crowded him in theatres, blocked and ran passes for him in bars, sat in on his dinners with new friends, sounded for him in banks and restaurants. His family constantly found reasons to come east and check up on him, bring him things, kiss him. I, who was to turn thirty before I dared embrace my father and have never done more than shake hands with my brothers, was dazzled. Still, I wondered how much protection one needs. Mac's friends insistently set him up with Good Husband Material; their dinner parties looked like the waiting room at Yenta the Matchmaker's. And Mac's family had their version, prodding him to Come Home and Settle Down—meaning, translated from the straight, "Give up the rebellious gay phase and do what is done."

But Mac loved the city. He loved crowds and dinners and doing eight things every evening. "Do you realize?" he had written in one of his earliest letters, "that there are probably a million gays in New York? Allowing for variables of looks, spirit, vocation, and bad habits, each of us may have a thousand ideal mates within immediate geography. We need but look."

What can you project without a voice in this town of the insinuating opener and the whipcrack reply? You might show optimism, hesitation, disappointment, pain—and all too clearly. Speakers grow up learning to develop or hide their emotions; Mac had learned only to display his. Thus did he speak, as he claimed. Better, he charmed. And I mean strang-

25

ers. Belligerent strangers. Even belligerent, tough strangers on a mean bad day.

I went walking with him one afternoon when he had just received news about an aunt who had cancer; like a puppy, Mac perked up when you walked him. I'm champion at distracting wounded comrades—when all else fails, I start a fight—but Mac was half in a daze, and blundered into fresh-laid concrete on Forty-ninth Street, east of Park. One of the masons, foully irate, came over to berate him. Before I could intervene with my usual exacerbating ruckus, Mac stopped me, indicating the laborer with the philosopher's upheld index finger and himself with a down-turned thumb.

"He's right and I'm wrong," I sounded, dubiously, for Mac. He showed us the sidewalk, ran a hand over his eyes, and chided the hand with a look. "I should have been watching where I was going."

As the laborer blankly surveyed this latest charade of the Manhattan streets, Mac tore off a message for him.

"'I have had bad news,'" the man read out. "'I'm sorry.'" He looked at Mac. "Family news, huh?"

Mac nodded.

"Yeah, well . . . yeah, sure." He shifted his stance and patted Mac's shoulder. "It'll be all right. I'm sorry, too. For yelling."

Mac hit his chest with a fist and shook his head. "No," I sounded. "It was my fault."

"No—"

Mac hit himself again.

"No." The man grabbed Mac by the shoulders. "No, you . . . look . . . I gotta get back to work." He touched Mac's nose and gave him a quarter. "Be a good boy, now."

Mac smiled and nodded.

"Right," I said, after we had walked on a bit. "I've been in New York for seven years and I've seen, I think, everything. But did that really happen?"

Mac shrugged benignly.

"*He gave you a quarter!*"

"People like me," Mac wrote. "I'm nice."

"What's the secret of nice?" I wondered aloud.

"Forgiving," he wrote.

He could have used somewhat more in height and weight, no doubt; it doesn't do to be quite so boyish after twenty-six. Yet he made it work, for his short and thin suited the grin and the nod. He was the kind of man who could grow a moustache and no one would notice—would see it, even. He was the eternal kid, tirelessly seeking his mate. Fastidious, he wanted true love or nothing. But love is scarce even when forgiveness makes you nice, and I wondered what Mac did to fill in meanwhile, till one afternoon when Dennis Savage and I were hacking around in Mac's apartment and Mac pulled out the world's largest collection of porn magazines.

He did it, typically, to stop a war. Dennis Savage was cranky (as usual) and began to growl at me about something or other. Who knows, now, what? My taste in men? My dislike of travel? The Charge of the Light Brigade? Anyway:

"I'm going to get a huge dog," says Dennis Savage. "And you know what I'll train him to do?"

Mac touched us urgently, him then me. "Please don't fight," I sounded; adding, for myself, "Okay."

"Bite up your ass," Dennis Savage concluded.

"You don't need a dog for that, from what I hear."

He rose, fuming like Hardy when Laurel puts a fish in his pants, and Mac got between us, scribbling a cease-fire: "Sit down to play Fantasy." Bemused, we held our peace as he hauled stacks of magazines out of a closet. "I usually play by myself," he mimed to my sound, "but it works in groups, too." He handed us each a number, prime porn. "Browse and choose," he wrote. "Each gets anyone he wants for one night."

"Get him," said Dennis Savage.

Mac wrote a note just for him: "Pretend!"

"Where did all this porn come from?" I asked. "It's like the Decadent Studies Room in the Library of Congress."

Mac went through an elaborate mime. "I threw up on the bureau of my aunt?" suggested Dennis Savage.

Mac made a wry face as he picked up the pad. "It keeps me off the streets," he wrote.

"Strange men give him quarters," I added. "They touch his nose."

"He forgives," Dennis Savage noted, "and his kisses are as sweet as the bottom inch of a Dannon cup." Innocence is Dennis Savage's party.

Mac reverently showed us a spread entitled "The Boys of Soho." Writing "This one's my fave," he pointed out a dark-haired chap of about twenty-five, standing nude, arms folded across his stomach. There was nothing splendid about his looks or proportions, but something arresting somewhere; his face, you thought; you searched it, found nothing, but kept looking. Amid a load of musclemen, hung boys, and surly toughs, here was a man of no special detail but an attitude of sleaze too personable to ignore. I imagine evil looks like this.

"'Nick,'" I read out. "'A typical Soho boy with an air of fun and a taste for the finer things.' What does that mean, I wonder?"

"Hepatitus B on the first date," Dennis Savage answered.

Mac mimed, and I sounded: "Do you think he would respond to a letter?"

"Mac, you wouldn't fall in love with that! What would your family say?"

"Just for a night," Mac mimed, then, by pad: "How would you contact such a person?"

"We wouldn't know," said Dennis Savage, "so forget it."

"You could write him a letter in care of the photographer," I put in. "Or even call the photographer and ask—"

"You bonehead!" Dennis Savage pointed out.

"Let the kid have some fun. Why should he go through life only imagining where such paths lead? Everyone alive who isn't a coward or a creep deserves one glorious night."

"Which are you? Coward or creep?"

"Glorious."

28

He waved this nonsense away and concentrated on Mac. "I'm going to set you up with some very excellent Italian accountants in the West Seventies. They make the best husbands, believe me. Always remember The Three Advantages of the Italian beau: hairy chest, volcanic thighs, and the commitment of a Pope."

"*Volcanic thighs?*" I howled. "And dare I ask where the lava comes out?"

Slowly he turned. He regarded me. He was stern. "You know, you should take care where you go. Fag-bashing incidents have been reported in this area."

"Such as where?"

"Such as in this apartment in about three seconds."

"I dream of Nick," Mac had written, and now showed us his little pad. "I think it's always Nick."

"Another good boy goes wrong," said Dennis Savage. "Is that why you left Racine? To meet Nicks?"

Mac gazed at the photograph. "He's such a beautiful dude," I sounded, watching Mac's face.

"Will you shut up?" Dennis Savage roared.

"It wasn't me."

Porn models are surprisingly easy to meet—as if their photos were meant as credentials for work. Despite Dennis Savage's reservations, I helped Mac make contact with Nick. This was 1976, when dubious encounters were quaint adventure rather than mortal peril; so let the harmless fantasy come true for a night. Very little trouble yielded Nick's telephone number, and I made the call for Mac and set up an appointment. Nick sounded as one might have expected, trashy and agreeable. No, you wouldn't kick him out of bed—but you wouldn't want your brother to marry him. He wasn't in the least thrown to hear that his date couldn't talk.

"You should see some of the things I get with," he said. "Once I went to a meet and this guy had no legs." He laughed. "So whattaya think of that?"

Instinct warned me to arrange Mac's date for as soon as

possible; I did not picture Nick keeping a terribly precise engagement book.

"How about now?" he asked.

It was a Saturday afternoon and Mac was game, so we cinched it—but it worried me that he didn't want me to stay and set things up with Nick, not to mention check him out for weapons. I never heard of Mac's taking an adventure alone. But he was adamant. "This fantasy I must not share," he wrote. The urgency was unnerving.

Worse yet, Mac refused to tell how the date had gone. That he had had a wonderful time was unmissable; the grin was showing about twenty-five more teeth and the nod came a hair more slowly now, as if Mac had grown younger and wiser at once. Bits of dish would slide out of him perchance: Nick had spent the weekend at Mac's that first time; Nick lived in a hole in darkest Brooklyn; Nick was seeing Mac regularly at bargain rates; Nick was very pleasant under the mean-streets facade.

Suddenly Nick moved in with Mac.

Dennis Savage, when he heard, was shocked silent for a good two minutes, an ideal condition for him. Our Mac—so he had become, for to befriend him was to own him—consorting with sex-show debris? When Dennis Savage regained his voice, he went into a ten-minute tirade reproaching me for encouraging Mac in this vile stunt, for having the sensitivity of Mickey Spillane, and for living. How was I to know that a date with a hustler would yield romance? Whoever heard of the fantasy coming true? I had always thought hustlers were the ultimate tricks, guaranteed for one time only, impersonal and beyond reach. Would not fantasy begin to dissolve at the touch of real life? Why else is "the morning after" as terrible a term in gay as "no exit" is in hell?

Yet Mac's fantasy held. I saw it in the way he spoke of Nick and to him—and Nick, fascinated by the gestures of hand and face that made words for the rest of us, would stare in smug wonder and cry, "Go for it, sport! Go for it!"

Mac did, all the way. It was dinners with Nick, cinema

and hamburgers with Nick, Monopoly with Nick—the first American I've known, by the way, who couldn't play the game. You don't realize how broad our range of kind is here in the magic city till you meet someone who doesn't know what Monopoly is. I've played it with Ph.Ds and little kids, with the birthright wealthy and users of food stamps, with actors and construction workers, with competitors and nerds. Some had mastered it—to the point that they virtually knew where they would land when they were shaking the dice—and some learned by playing, and some were frankly not apt. But everyone knew what it was. Nick had never heard of it—could not, moreover, pick it up no matter how carefully we explained it. My friend Carlo, who likes just about everyone and has a superb ability to forgive hot men their little misdemeanors, walked home with me after this Monopoly game and, in a lull, pensively regarded the traffic and said, "Tell me, who was that extremely terrible boy?"

Mac's coterie shook their prickles at me for bringing Nick into his life, and, believe me, I did not rejoice. But the man was happy. No, he had always been happy; now he was cocky, getting around more by himself, doing what he wanted to on spunk, not on the assistance of his chorus of Rolfs. I found myself sounding, again and again, "I am glad," for him. I hear tell of a chemistry bonding the socioeconomically energetic with the intellectually needy: yet what lies below Baltic Avenue?

I learned what at one of Mac's dinners. He was held up at the office again, and the other guests, respectably employed, could be reached at their places of business and told to come along later. But I had been out mooching around in the streets, viewing the town for adaptable incidents, and so arrived for the party before I should have: when Nick was alone.

"This fantasy I must not share" ran through my mind that evening, as the Theme of Alberich's Curse runs through *Der Ring des Nibelungen*. And there before me was a kind of Al-

31

berich, the dark lord, wearing nothing but navy blue corduroy pants held up by suspenders. Just as Nick was ignorant of this nation's essential board game, so was he a gracelessly unknowing host. He offered nothing, not even a chair. He said nothing, not even about Mac being held up. He seemed to regard me as if I were a movie: he paid complete attention without doing anything himself.

I went into the kitchen and poured myself some wine. When I came out, he was where he had been, spread out on the sofa, idly shifting a suspender arm from the curve of his left pectoral to the nipple and back again.

"So whattaya say?" he finally uttered.

What does one say to the kind of man who looks naked in pants? "How does it feel" was what I came up with, "to switch from free-lancing to a steady position?"

"Yeah."

"You don't miss the scene?" Living as I did along Hustler Alley on East Fifty-third Street, I had seen the dire fascination that brought certain of Nick's colleagues back to the neighborhood night after night, some restively pushing the agenda early of a Saturday or dully clinging to the illusion as the sun came up on Sunday. Passing by with my groceries or my playbill, I had the impression that they had nothing but this for life, that the success of a paying rendezvous was less important than the simple fact of membership in the club of hot.

"Miss the scene?" Nick repeated. "I miss it like my last case of crabs."

"Ah."

"Miss the scene?" He laughed. "I could tell you about that. I could *tell* about the *scene!*" He laughed again. "You know what they are?"

"Who?"

"They're garbage is what. They'd rob blind cripples."

"Don't you have to stay in touch with your clients?"

"My what?"

"Your regulars. The johns."

"Oh. *Wallets.*"

"That's what you call them?"

"That's what they are. Money. Talking money. Asshole money. Fat, drooling money, and hair all over it like stupid. What do I want with them now? I got a deal here. I can sleep late. No hassle. I can do like . . . anything. And then Mac comes home and makes me feel good. Little Mac. He makes those cute things with his hands. He cooks dinner. All I have to do is lay him nice and easy. Sometimes they like it when you hurt them, you know? But Little Mac likes it lullaby-style."

"He makes you feel good?"

"You bet. Like when he smiles if you put your arm around him. He feels nice. You know, he's pretty. A pretty little nice boy. You know that kind? I like to feel him up. Tickle him, you know? Watch him shake. That's real dandy. I make him dance. Did he ever dance for you? Real pretty, when they dance. So pretty. He's not like a wallet and he's not like dig. You know?"

"Dig?"

"Dig is what I am. A wallet pays a dig, right?" He toyed with his suspender again. "Oh, what's he like, now? He's like a brother I had once. Kid brother. I made him dance, too. But like who could tickle a wallet, you know?"

"Dig is what you are."

"He should go pro. Let me turn him out. We could make two hundred a night, easy. These East Side wallets, they've got these videos? Pay you anything to make tape for them. They like tell you this story and then you do it. Acting. Maybe I'll be an actor, right? But the best thing I do is dance video. That's my hottest." He sat up.

"Dance video?"

"Mac'd be good at that, too. I like to dance. I like to fuck and dance. You got video? You want to make some tape, now? Bargain rates, 'cause you're a friend. We'll make one together, you know? Anything you want. Anything."

I looked at him. It was quite a long moment.

"What's with those shades, anyway? You doing something bad?"

He took hold of my glasses at the bridge and pulled them off. "Uh-oh." He replaced them. "No video. Gotcha." He laughed. "The man doesn't dance. The man does *not* choose to dance."

"Not with the likes of you."

He stopped laughing. "You got the eyes of a cop."

I've witnessed various liaisons with hustlers over the years, the street kind as well as the call-boy elite, on a dating and live-in basis; each has ended differently. One hustler drifts out of reach like a balloon in the park, another dwindles into a sexless chum, one vanishes, another gets pushy about money or moves on into his host's coterie or turns lawless and ends in jail. I even know of one—I'll get to him some pages hence—who was thrown out by a man who couldn't live with perfection. Nick adds another trope to the catalogue: the fuck machine plugged into a good gig, he simply hung on. Mac's friends fretted and his visiting brothers scowled, but something like a year went by and everyone but Mac was still waiting for Nick to clear out. Dennis Savage thumbed his black book to tatters manifesting Italian accountants, and dinners were duly arranged. But it was the dark lord whom the accountants loved, not the mute boy. Like it or not, Nick was hot.

So it stayed Mac and Nick, though no one ever tied them verbally, out of fear of giving their duet legitimacy. I think most gays respect the mating of twins, not the sharing of fantasy. Mac had offended custom, and this sin above all bills its dues. And Mac paid, when somebody with money beckoned to Nick.

It hit suddenly, at another dinner—perhaps my thousandth in New York, and never have I been given enough to eat—and Dennis Savage and I arrived to find Nick throwing clothes into a backpack as Mac followed him around frantically signaling.

"I know when it's time," Nick philosophized for our benefit. "It's time for L.A. Because I hate this fucking snow, and bartenders, and niggers on bicycles—"

Mac grabbed my arms, pointed to Nick, then hugged himself, watching me with huge asking eyes.

"I don't know what you're saying," I told him.

"This guy saw me in Studio, right? He dropped his glasses on the dance floor and who picks them up?"

"A wallet," I said.

"No, he's okay. I'm going back with him. On a *plane!*"

Mac moved to Nick, indicating their faces, their hearts, trying to smile. Nick turned away, muttering, "Sure, sure," but Mac took his hand and touched it to Nick's forehead.

Nick jerked his hand away. "Make him stop that stuff."

"After what he's done for you, my friend," said Dennis Savage, "the least you should—"

"Hey," said Nick, his arms as wide as his smile, slurring the word out the way grown-ups do when talking to children, "I earned it, didn't I?" He patted Mac's head and headed for the door. "Stay loose, boys," he called out. "And remember our motto: 'Don't screw anything made of wood.'" He laughed and pulled open the door as Mac ran up, pencil dashing across the top leaf of a pad. He tore it off and handed it to Nick.

"Give it to the next guy," said Nick. He crumpled the note, let it fall, and closed the door behind him.

Mac stayed where he was, facing the door, shaking his head. Finally he turned, touched his eyes, indicated us, and militantly brushed his palm across the air.

"I don't want you to see me cry," I sounded.

"We've seen you smile so much," said Dennis Savage. "I don't think a little crying would hurt."

Mac shook his head, holding back the tears. We didn't move, and he shook his head again.

I took the pad and pencil from him, and wrote, "Would you like a quarter?"

He read it, reclaimed the kit, and wrote, "It hurts to be nice."

I furiously shook my head.

He nodded grimly.

Dennis Savage held him very, very gently from behind, as if afraid of being pushed away. "Come on and cry," he urged. He had picked up the crumpled note, and put it in Mac's hand and closed his fist around it.

Mac looked at me.

"What?" I said.

He handed me the note. I opened it. It read, "My aunt died today."

"Mac," I said, "why did you write this?"

That was when he began to cry.

Mac went home for the funeral, returned to New York, and, bare weeks after, went back to Wisconsin on a long vacation. Letters poured out, somewhat less ebullient than usual; or perhaps as ebullient, but about unusual things—the nightingales at his window or losing to his nephew at chess. He would sneak back to the city, not calling any of us—Mac, the most intent comrade of all. How dare the little bastard, I thought, spotting him in the D'Agostino midway between our apartments. He's supposed to be in Racine! At least he had the sense of style to be embarrassed, which made it worse. I followed him to the checkout line, and sounded for him to the clerk: he had forgotten to take his pad. This is like forgetting to wear your shoes in a blizzard.

The Racine trips grew longer, but Mac continued to write. However, the letters grew shorter.

"Is it Nick?" I asked Dennis Savage. "All this mourning because a love affair ended?"

"Where do you get off reducing it to 'all this mourning'? Who are you to point a finger—you who set it all up, as I recall?"

"I hate you for that."

"And you aren't joking."

36

"I was helping! How was I to know that Mac could stay intrigued by a Nick?"

"Who made you the social arbiter of gay romance?"

"It was supposed to be one glorious night. *One*. It does *not* follow that a . . . a player of Monopoly would want to coexist with someone who can't tell a house from a hotel!"

He looked pensive. "Who knows less about love than you? The Wicked Witch of the West?"

"All right, what happens now? Is Mac's life ruined because that slimy hustler busted his heart? No doubt you know much of one, true, life-long love—no one I know has been in and out of it more variously than you."

"Jeers from a left-out."

"So tell me: can it destroy as surely as it exhilarates?"

"We must watch developments," he replied. "We must see and know."

Developments proved invisible, for Mac gave up his apartment and resettled in Wisconsin. Odd letters trickled back, drab ones now. Mac's mail used to soar. He never mentioned Nick, though there were what I took as oblique references, in phrases like "the fantasies of Manhattan" or "the grip of wishes." I would respond with carefree dish and, perhaps two months later, back would come another feeble laudamus of rustic places. "More and more," he wrote, "I have come to appreciate the plain heart of the midwest." I felt as if he had spit on me.

I continued to write, as breezily as I could manage. There was pleasant news: Lionel was teaching at the New School, Carlo lucked into a job at a ritzy boutique and became solvent for the first time since grade school, Eric sold his first novel to a major house, Dennis Savage had met a dazzling young man in, of all places, the Forty-Sixth Street Theatre, and the boy was so pure it took our Circuit paragon four dates to bed him. Are Manhattan's fantasies so blameful, then? We were all pushing thirty, and great dreams were slipping within our reach. And so I said to Mac, straight out: "Some fantasies must be shared."

Mac never answered; his wife did, enclosing photographs of the wedding. Her name was Patricia; she had known Mac all their lives, and had married Mac's high-school buddy, one of the last American casualties in Vietnam. Shortly after his death, Patricia had given birth to their son, Ty. A very midwestern story. I saw them all in the pictures: Pat quite pretty, Ty a handsome and sombre little boy, and the Mac I had known in New York, glad and lively. And still believing in fantasy. A thousand McNallys surrounded them, held them, admired them. There was even a tiny Ty with the model couple atop the festive cake. "And Mac," Patricia ended, "is a natural-born father. We put on a record of 'The Parade of the Tin Soldiers' and Mac and Ty march around the room. You should see little Ty, how seriously he takes it. There is so much love in the world, I cannot know why I have been so lucky." And she closed with, "Your friend, Patricia McNally."

I never heard from Mac again.

I did see Nick, though, some years later, in some other spread in some other magazine. What, *Cockstorm? Bullstick?* And the spread—"Fantasy Boys"? It might as well have been. Nick was fondling a younger man, who gazed up at him in tender terror. No doubt Nick was making him dance. I was in a room full of men at party, and they passed the magazine from hand to hand to see.

"My God, that one's hot!" someone exclaimed.

"How . . . hot . . . is he?" said another, in the cue-up style of Ed McMahon.

"He's so hot," said the jester, "he could make a straight turn gay."

I let it pass.

The Homogay

These stories, reader, are meant as mine in particular, not as gay stories in general—not depictions per se. Each life bears its own tales. Still, I am concerned at how often people cry in these pages. Life is not that sad. I've made up my mind that there will be no crying in this one.

I come from a town so small that every mother's son is born at home in mother's bed. So small the school bus made but three stops. So small the bully had to double as the sissy.

His name was Harvey Jonas. He had a high-pitched voice, his frame carried a pudding of blubber, and he was a fiasco at sports: the classic adolescent queer. Yet he was intently aggressive, even sadistic, especially with those smaller than he: a classic adolescent tormentor. I frankly admit I was afraid of him. With a little warning, anyone could outrun him, but sometimes he would lie in wait, then come hurtling out to nab you, braying like a monstrous donkey. Once he caught me while I was pumping my bicycle tires and, without uttering a word, snatched the air pump and marched off with it.

Our meanest encounter happened up by the swings one summer evening. Harvey came upon me and my two little brothers while we were in the air and couldn't run off. Anyway, you can't run in front of little brothers. I stood my ground and had the first extrafamilial fight of my life, outclassed by Harvey's superior weight and a warrior's will I had yet to develop. My brothers came to my aid—Andrew socked his head and Tony bit his foot—but I was losing badly until my older brother Jim happened by.

Jim was one of those cooly murderous youths who, if not strangled at birth, grow up to comprise a sizable fraction of the straight male population as cooly murderous adults. I must admit, though, that it was rather grand knowing him on this occasion. Always decisive if sloppy on the amenities, Jim grabbed Harvey by the hair and swung him with a grunt into one of the metal posts that supported the swings. Harvey lay where he landed, and I feared he might be dead, but suddenly he reared up and ran off. At a safe distance, he turned around and brayed at us.

"That," Jim observed with disgust, "is one champion queer."

"Yeah," I said.

"He sure is," agreed Andrew.

"I bit his foot," said Tony.

"And you know what you are?" Jim asked me, getting around to one of his favorite subjects. "A stupid *jerk*." He shoved me. "Because you can't even defend yourself from a *fag* with an *army* to help you!"

"I bit his foot," said Tony.

Jim shoved me again. "Because you were *born* a jerk and you'll *die* a jerk!" He stared at me as if he could see another Harvey Jonas on the rise. I was there; I know it; I can feel how it looks to this day. And Jim stalked off.

It's tricky being the middle child: half the known world looks up to you and the other half looks down. Andrew and Tony waited for the next move, but I was too crushed to initiate anything.

"Do you want us to grunch his room for you?" asked Andrew, to cheer me up. "Grunch" is to ruin, to trash.

"The Revolt of the Moon Mice!" cried Tony, planning the marquee. "Let's chew Jujubes and dribble them in his sneakers!"

Childhood is hard. I'll skip ahead now to my grownup years in New York—you'll see why directly—to a fey and raucous party of gays and their friends in the West Nineties. I knew no one; the other guests all seemed to be old comrades. There was a lot of liquor and smoke and by midnight the place was roaring. A few couples were openly smooching, a Puerto Rican teenager was wandering around wearing nothing but a Melitta coffee filter paper around his middle (it was large and he was small), and, in the main room, two queens were doing show-biz impersonations.

It appeared to be a set routine. After a handsome actor type smoothly intoned into an imaginary microphone, "And now, it's time for *Dish Maven,* with the first legend of stage and screen, Miss Katharine Hepburn," seven or eight people hummed "Fine and Dandy"—*Dish Maven*'s theme song, I guessed. And "Hepburn," on a couch, ran through the rituals of the talk show, with preposterous commercials, rampant plugola, and unwitting egotism.

"And now, Miss Hepburn," the actory announcer cut in, "it's time to bring on your special guest."

"Damn. I was just going to do *Coco* medley," said Kate.

"Too late now, for here comes your dearest friend and competitor, the scintillant Miss Bette Davis!"

To a reprise of "Fine and Dandy," a second queen joined Kate on the couch, eyeing her as Hamlet might eye King Lear.

"Deah, deah Kate!" rasped Bette.

"Miss Davis' clothes," Kate told the crowd, "designed exclusively by K-Mart fashions!"

"Who is older, Kate?" Bette asked. "You or the Gobi Desert?"

"Quick!" Kate cried to an imaginary orchestra. "*Coco* medley!"

"*Coco?*" asked Bette. "I pronounce it with cedillas: *Soso!*"

"Well, you never won an Oscar!"

"You slept with Howard Hughes!"

"You made *Beyond the Forest!*"

"Ladies, ladies!" urged the announcer. "Surely you great

survivors can stop feuding and tell us of Hollywood's golden age."

The two stars fell into each other's arms. "We'll reminisce!" Kate swore; and Bette was overwhelmed. "Yes," Kate went on, "yes, we knew them all: Gable, Hank Fonda, dear little Deanna Durbin, sweet as halvah. And, of course, Bette, I had my marvelous Spencer and you had no one, but they were great, great times!"

"I had William Wellman."

"I want to ask you a very important question, Bette. Now, it may seem academic—and I know our guests are waiting for golden-age dish—but, seriously, Bette . . . you knew them all. The directors, the writers—"

"Such as F. Scott Fitzpatrick, my favorite, who wrote *Tender Are the Damned!*"

". . . the actors . . . and you knew what greatness was, as I did, and you knew the beauty of the art. You knew it! You *knew* it!" It was like Hepburn in *The Lion in Winter,* running, mounting, soaring. "Griffith and Gish! *Gone With the Wind!* The comebacks and the glory! And what I want to ask you is . . ."

"Yes?"

"Who had the biggest boner in Hollywood?"

And of course everyone laughed and clapped, and someone cried in a Tallulah voice, *"I* did, dahling!," and people refilled their glasses, and I was bowled over. I had come to New York for fast-moving hip, freedom from straights, and a touch of dada; here they all were at once. While musing on this, I suppose, I was unconsciously staring at the man who had played Hepburn. He was tall, not good-looking, and strikingly weightlifted; another year or two of iron and he could have entered a contest. The contrast between his physique and his performance was like a standoff between homosexuality as a feeling and gay as a style, the clipped hunk look warring with the camp. Half of him was more homo than gay, the other half more gay than homo. He was *homogay;* and he was, I suddenly noticed, aware that I was looking at him. He came over, posed, and said in a sultry voice through Jane Russell lips, "They call me Lorinda."

"That was expert satire," I told him. "You got television, Hollywood, and show-biz megalomania all at once."

He was looking at me oddly; was I too stiff for this party? "Go on," he said, in his own voice. "Say something else."

"Why?"

"Because I know you."

"No, you don't," I told him, strangely fearful.

"It's Bud Mordden, isn't it?"

"Who are you?"

"So!" he screamed, Lorinda again. People were looking. "Have you forgotten that night in romantic Mahony City when you pledged to be true?"

It was Harvey Jonas. Most gays conquer an atrocious childhood by going either completely virile or completely fag. Harvey had done both. No wonder I hadn't recognized him: he was twice disguised. Nearly speechless, I said the first thing that hit me: "You stole my bicycle pump."

"But not your heart, I see." He squeezed my thigh and "whispered," "What are you doing after the game, fullback? Let me teach you some new positions." More people were looking, and I backed away from him.

"Slow down," I said.

"A hometown girl like me needs her sweetheart by her side!" He was screaming again; now half the party was watching, including, inches away, the Puerto Rican in the Melitta filter. Briskly switching over to Eve Arden, Harvey told the boy, "You have an emergency call—coffee for three in Room 308," turned him around and pushed him away. "They'll want plenty of hot cream from your spigot, too," he added, and turned back to me.

"Now, my old friend," he said, in quiet, even, masculine tones, grasping my shoulders. "Let's understand each other vividly. If you tell a single soul . . . and I mean *anyone*: a judge, a ribbon clerk, a bag lady . . . if you tell anyone about my past, I swear I'll rip you apart, limb from limb." Grasping harder, he flexed his right biceps. "Feel that."

"No, I'll take your word for it." Twenty years after, the same bully was still harassing me.

"If you're nice to me," he added, softening, "I'll be nice to you. Silence?"

"All right."

"Will you shake hands on it, in our simple country way?"

"No. But I'll give you my word."

He regarded me for a bit, then nodded. "I'll trust you."

Suddenly a voice rang out: "Auditions for the chorus line! Auditions for the *Hello, Dolly!* number!" Harvey swept back into the throng; now he was Carol Channing. "And *I'm* Dolly!" he announced. "Hello, everybody!"

"Hello, Carol!" they replied. And that day at the swings, which I had almost succeeded in burying, came flooding back into me like poison.

I would have been glad to give Harvey a wide berth, but for some reason he adopted me. He was utterly uninterested in me physically and we were not compatible as friends; however, he often included me in a crowd. I went along because I liked his crowd; after all, I had come to New York to join it. And never once did he revert to the threat he had voiced that night we reconvened. He had learned to project his toughness at genuine enemies, from impedient bureaucrats to sullen doormen, casually and fiercely. He was shameless. A scene in a bank or restaurant energized him. One minute he would be regaling the dinner table with his Tallulah and Carol; the next, he'd have a flippant waiter by the hair threatening to wash his face in soup if he didn't snap to. And he meant it; and he was over two hundred pounds of total beef.

He could be very funny. Once, in his apartment, he performed a version of *A Little Night Music* with Bette Davis in the lead, bungling the lyrics, quoting lines from her films, haranguing the audience with homophobic paranoia. He did Hal Prince, shaping Concept Production. He did Sondheim, tear-ing his hair. He did Kate Hepburn, sneaking into the show during "A Weekend in the Country" and trying to usurp Bette's role. I was literally on the floor, holding my stomach and screaming for mercy.

He was popular but loveless: the face was wrong. He worked out at Sheridan Square but, on the street, never nodded to the others who did, as most of them do. He scarcely cruised at all. His queen act centered on romance and sex; in real life, he stepped around them. There were times, rare ones when we were alone together, when I thought he was about to say something intimately sad, *homo,* but then he would cut over to some slashing line, *gay,* like, "You want hot truth? Love is so stupid they should give it to straights" or "I'm loud and crass and that's my fun—love me or leave me!"

One spends the first years in New York collecting coterie, one's next years trimming it. I moved on to a crowd in a lower key, given to ties and quiet pricey restaurants. At L'Aiglon one night I told them about Harvey's routines and they just looked at each other blankly. (It was a dull group, but the clothes were fun.) I kept in touch with Harvey and told him of my doings, and he became fascinated by the company I kept. They had names like Crosby and Raymond and were smooth operators. In their gentle way they made good stories, and in his rowdy way Harvey took them into his act. "Bette Meets Crosby," he would announce, then show me how the diva fared among the townhouse gentry. The adventure varied with his mood. "Tea is served," he once narrated, enacting it, "and Bette deftly raises a pinkie. But the potent tea has unaccountably excited her, and she finds to her horror that she has erected a *tremendous boner* just as Lady Fashionbury leans over to enquire after her health!"

He stopped and looked at me. "We aren't close, are we?"

I said nothing. It always unnerved me when he went into his own voice.

"Still, I'm going to ask a favor of you. If you say no, we won't mention it again, all right?" He came over to me, smiling. "I want to come along with you to one of those dinners you have with your gentlemen friends. The Crosby gang. Harvey Meets Crosby. Yes or no?"

"Well . . . actually . . ."

He waited, towering above me. "Yes or no?" He grabbed my arm and pulled me to my feet. I saw the swings again, and my brothers fighting alongside me and Jim hating me. "Just say yes or no."

"Yes or no."

He let me go and moved away. Then he roared with laughter. "How's your love life?" he asked.

"Fine."

"You never speak of it."

"I keep secrets."

"Yes, I'm well aware. You keep a good secret. Do you ever think about . . . back then?"

"You know," I said, "I'd rather direct this scene than be in it, but I wouldn't know what to tell the actors. What is this scene about?"

"Why won't you take me to meet the Crosby gang?"

"Because you threatened me."

"Is that the only reason?"

I lied. "Yes."

"You want hot truth? I don't even want to meet them. I truly don't. I'd just make them angry, wouldn't I? I'd dip my spoon into the fingerbowl and say, 'What delicious consommé!' And, tasting my pheasant, I'd turn to Crosby and say, 'It's absolu de*lish!*' No, I wouldn't say it. I'd *scream* it, right there in Le Grand Can-Can or wherever it is you go to." And he did scream it, right there in his apartment. "Absolu de*lish!* It's *ab*solu de*lish!*" He paced and frumped like Davis in her Elizabeth movies. "Why, Layt-ty Crospy, how haugh-ty you seem tto-ttay!" He pushed me back down on the couch. The damned aren't always tender. He was furious—not, I think, at me. "They all have lovers, don't they, the Crosby gang?"

"No, not all. A few. Nothing long-lasting."

"That type doesn't need lovers, anyway. They have fuck chums." This too he screamed out. *"Fuck!Chums!* Once a month, with the lights turned down and a little Mozart in the background. Oh, it's delicate and soigné. I'll bet they don't even fuck. Fuck is too lewd for that coven. They *cuddle!"* He sat down across the room from me and kicked off his shoes, calming down. "That brother of yours, the handsome one . . . Jim. He's gay, isn't he?"

"No."

"You're wrong."

"No, I'm not."

Harvey pulled off his socks and threw them in a corner.

I cleared my throat. "What *is* this scene about, by the way?"

"The scene is about how to hold a lover. Do you want a lover? Don't answer; almost everyone does. Almost everyone." He began to unbutton his shirt. "You're my oldest friend and you know my secrets. Not all of them. But some of the best ones. Now let me tell you how to hold your beautiful gay lover. By being terrific in bed? No. That will guarantee a good premiere, but beautiful lovers by nature have already had much taste of fabulous carnal technique. You won't hold him that way. Am I making you nervous?" He got up and slowly peeled off his shirt. "What else? By having pecs or thighs of death? No. Who doesn't, nowadays?" He unbuckled his belt, opened his pants, and took them off. Nude, he presented the most spectacular member I've ever seen. A bit longer or heavier and it would have been grotesque; like so, it was . . . well, champion queer. "Cock of death, too, has been called premium. But cock, I've discovered, is made for tricking, not love. Oh yes . . . yes, how often you've heard a man sigh that cock is everything. Once you've been fucked by a big one you can never go back to the minor leagues. Have you heard this?" He stroked himself fleetingly. "I've seen men weep as they lay before me, vulnerable and poetic, waiting for me to begin. They weep for joy. For a moment, one imagines that nothing else in the world is as important as cock. The wonder of it! But they don't stay. They don't take you in their arms and just hold on so quietly and happily. They don't look at you, at any time of day, with those wild eyes one hears tell of. They don't need you. Nor, I'm sorry to say, will wit or social grace avail you. No, there is only one way to hold a lover: by having a handsome face. You may have noticed that I do not. Not partly or nearly. Not *possibly*. And once one isn't handsome, one never will be. Everyone talks about power, but everyone wants beauty. It's sad, because you can acquire power but you can't acquire beauty. Do you know why everyone wants beauty? Because beauty is the only thing in the world that isn't a lie."

He extended his arms, palms outward. "I am not offering myself to you, incidentally. I simply wish to show you, as generously as possible, a choice irony of contemporary urban life. Would you ever so mind going now?"

I got up. At the door he said, his eyes on the floor, "Somewhat needless to say, if you tell anyone about this . . ."

"I'm not afraid of you anymore."

He looked up. "Were you ever?"

"All my life. Till about five minutes ago."

He opened the door, then gently pulled me back as he thought of something. "Tell me, where is your brother now?"

"Here. He lives a few blocks from me, in fact."

"What would happen if you said hello to him for me?"

"I haven't spoken to Jim in years."

He considered this. "You always had a very strange family. What was that littlest one's name?"

"Tony. He bit your foot."

Naked in the doorway, he watched me wait for the elevator. "That was all a long, long time ago," he said. "You can forgive me now."

"No, I can't. And I never will."

"Was I that awful to you?"

"It wasn't just you."

"Who else?"

I shook my head.

48

"It's ancient history," he urged. "An old story."

"This story isn't finished yet."

"If you're nice to me, I'll be nice to you."

I just looked at him and he shrugged and closed his door. So who did have the biggest boner in Hollywood? Harvey Jonas did, for all the good it did him; and it did him none; and that's fine with me. You want hot truth? That scene was about the ruin promoted by childhood calamaties. About how something goes wrong in infancy and nothing feels right thereafter. About being haunted by nameless worries.

I promised not to expose the secrets of Harvey Jonas. But he owes me satisfaction: for my bicycle pump, for what happened at the swings, and mainly for some other matter that I'd rather not mention just now.

There is no crying anywhere in this story.

The Precarious Ontology
of the Buddy System

Thinking back on the couples I have known, I note how many of them were unsuited for each other—Alex and Joe, for instance, or Mac and Nick. What is surprising about the gay fascination for the misalliance is how many odd couples actually seem rather made for each other, once they hook up. I marvel. When Dennis Savage, that very exponent of Stonewall-era sexual cosmopolitanism, picked up a youngster at standing room for *The Best Little Whorehouse in Texas,* I took it as usual news, at best a passing headline: ALLURING VETERAN NABS NEW BOY IN TOWN. But this was the boy it took four dates to land, and when their spotty rendezvous schedule grew constant, then insistent, I stood by, amused and supportive. When I met the boy and found him very young, very silly, and very uneducated, I held my peace. And when I saw this archon of the Circuit, the notable (if fiercely flawed) Dennis Savage, become so involved with this boy that he began to lecture me on the evils of the single-person family (especially mine), I smiled. One must. But then this kid moved in with Dennis Savage, and the kid was called Little Kiwi, and Dennis Savage acted as if he owned every place Little Kiwi was in, like a father, a creditor, and a king all at once. What was I to do? Especially as they would show up at my apartment whenever they chose. Actually, what I did was: I thought, There is a tale in this now. Another story begins to stir in this our gay life.

As Lord Mayor of the Circuit, Dennis Savage intends his visits as an honor, but somehow he always shows up when I'm pushing a deadline and, as he lives in my building, there's never a warning. If I bar my door to him, he goes into some grotesque routine in the hall, which makes for crabby neighbors. Worse yet, now that Little Kiwi has moved in with him, they go everywhere together, often in the company of Little Kiwi's disreputable dog, Bauhaus. But people tell me how lucky I am to have Dennis Savage's confidence—"and that fetching number who walks in his shadows! My, my, *my!*" Will you listen to the sound of them? As if we were still in the late 1940s, when all the bars were unmarked and only bombers wore bomber jackets.

I've told Dennis Savage to call first. I've lectured him on the rudeness of poking into my fridge uninvited. I've warned him that Little Kiwi's fabled charm is lost on me. And all he says is, "Have you noticed how lamplight picks up the tones in his hair?"

"How old is that kid, anyway?" I once asked him.

"Old enough to love."

"He has the interests of a child of eight."

"He voted in the last election."

"For whom? The Velveteen Rabbit?"

"Everyone adores him. They dress up for him and bake a pie. Look at you." I keep house in jeans and a sweatshirt. "And what do you give us to eat? BLTs!"

Actually, I give Dennis Savage BLTs. Little Kiwi subsists on grilled-cheese sandwiches and sliced tomato.

"Everyone wants Little Kiwi," says Dennis Savage. "You should know this. Except no one can have him but me."

"Oh, yeah?"

Dennis Savage chuckles. "I dare you."

How satisfying it would be to outfox Dennis Savage, though on the other hand his relationship with Little Kiwi is too fascinating to menace. I always listen for the sour notes in the gay duet, perhaps because the local Sloan's, at First Avenue and Fifty-third Street, seems at times to be populated exclusively by quarreling moustaches. But in these two I see the seamless fraternity of the worldly and the naïve, the hip and the unspoiled. Dennis Savage has been everywhere; Little Kiwi knows nothing.

Despite my complaints, I enjoy their visits, though they do tend to take over. One evening, as spring gave way to summer and my workday dwindled into daydreams and staring out the window, the two of them and Bauhaus paraded in. Dennis Savage went into the kitchen to see about a snack, Little Kiwi was poking into the two huge cardboard boxes my new stereo had come in, and Bauhaus grabbed a sneaker in his mouth, ran around in a craze, crashed into the piano, and lay there.

"Hey! This would make a great boat," said Little Kiwi, laying one of the boxes on the floor. "Would somebody push me around in my boat?"

"I'll push you, little darling," I said. Suddenly Dennis Savage came roaring out of the kitchen, steel in his eyes.

"Well, well, well," I remark. "Look at somebody nervous about something."

Dennis Savage takes a long breath and smiles. "This is a funny apartment and you are a funny man."

"It's a funny world."

"How would you like no head?"

"Now I'm playing store," Little Kiwi announces, hauling the box up on its side. "Who wants to buy a dog?"

"What else do you sell in your store?" I ask. "Kisses?"

Little Kiwi looked at me for quite some time, then shot the same look at Dennis Savage: confusion? distrust? fear? I must admit, lamplight does rather pick up the tones in his hair.

"You know," I said to Dennis Savage. "I think it's time you and I took Little Kiwi to the Island."

"What island?" Little Kiwi asked.

"Fire."

"Could Bauhaus come?"

"Surely," I replied. "What's Fire Island without Bauhaus?"

52

"I'm going to pack!" Little Kiwi cried, racing out with the dog.

"It so happens," says Dennis Savage, "that I had just such a trip in mind."

"Of course," I agreed. "Of course. Of course. Of course."

"But since you brought it up, you can make the arrangements."

"My pleasure."

"It'll be grand showing Little Kiwi all the places. Like revisiting our youth. There are three memories that every gay lives on—the first Gay Pride March, the first sight of the Saint, and the first trip to the Pines."

"Aren't you afraid of losing Little Kiwi out there?" I asked. "It's been known to happen."

He nodded, smiling vaguely, nodded again. "I've got Little Kiwi all wired down."

"You didn't seem to think so a minute ago. You came rocketing out of the kitchen like a husband."

"I just didn't want to miss anything," he said airily. "You put on such an amusing act. Yea, if I'm the husband, what are you—the iceman?"

"Maybe."

"Make sure you set us up in a real *bijou* of a house, now. We want to do the Island in top style."

"Shall we say the weekend after Memorial Day?"

"I can't wait to see Little Kiwi on the ferry—the wind in his hair and such. We could arrive just in time for tea and step right off the boat into the throng, Little Kiwi a sensation in lederhosen and I, Lord Mayor of the Circuit, greeting my fans." He regarded me with something like scorn. "Do you suppose you could, just for once, try to look famous? Nothing spoils an entrance like one of the party clomping in like somebody's uncle."

As he reached the door I said, "Please, don't worry about Little Kiwi and me."

53

"Was I planning to?"

"You know what they say about the iceman."

"What do they say, you bum sheik?"

"He cometh."

It went off like a dream. We claimed the hospitality of a wealthy friend of mine with a house on the surf, two decks, a pool, endless room, and the honest generosity of a golden-age host. We caught the Islanders' bus at Fifty-third and Second, Bauhaus and all, and Dennis Savage planted Little Kiwi across the aisle from us on his own. "He has to get out in the world," said Dennis Savage. There Little Kiwi entranced an elderly man with Wacko the Puppet, a character Little Kiwi creates by smushing his hand into a paper envelope to form a mouth. Wacko speaks in a crackly voice suggestive of Wheat Chex coughing and hasn't a shred of wit; his charm lies not in what he says but in the fact that Little Kiwi gets such a kick out of him. It's like Joan Crawford's acting: you don't admire the talent; you admire the commitment.

"I have a beautiful home on the bay," the old man was saying. "I'm looking for a houseboy. Would you like the job?"

"Don't do windows!" Wacko warned Little Kiwi.

"The duties are light," the man went on.

"That lets Little Kiwi out," Wacko observed. "He likes a lot of structure in his life."

"The salary is very negotiable."

"Now, Wacko," said Little Kiwi, "tell the folks that story about the Polish elephant."

"Please," the man pleaded. "Please."

"Why don't you trade seats with Little Kiwi?" I asked Dennis Savage. "He's shattering the social contract."

"He has to see life and learn. He's been very sheltered till now."

"He's about to give that old man a heart attack."

"That is the role that old men play in the gay world. If

54

you haven't accepted that by now, you'll never know any-thing."

As we disembarked at Sayville, Dennis Savage got teary. "Remember?" he kept saying. "Remember? The magic of the Island!" As the boat pulled out of the slip, he gripped Little Kiwi's shoulders and promised him the most spectacular experience of his life. Wacko immediately bit his nose and he calmed down; but, true enough, the spell of the Pines came upon us as we cut through the bay.

"There is a tale," I began. "In ancient days, when the Pines consisted of a few cottages and the ferries stopped once a week, a collection of very special people sped over the water to the Star Party. Everyone would come as a Hollywood personality, full kit. The food! The prizes! The guests! This was a festival to redeem an era!"

Mention elitism and all gays are transfixed. "When was this?" Dennis Savage asked. "Was Wacko there?" said Little Kiwi. "The puppet?"

"With so many stupendous guests, it was agreed that all would enter at the same moment. Consider them boarding the ferry, each thinking of his personal *grandezza,* retouching his *toilette,* planning his *mots.* Each had a secret dream of who he might be, could he but *become.*"

"The magic of the Island!" Dennis Savage breathed.

"What a tension there was as each came unto the ferry, the many dog-pets—impressed by the crush of celebrity—barking and whining." Little Kiwi patted Bauhaus' head; Bauhaus growled. "As the ferry neared the Island, the company tensed, wondered, thrilled. Consider their state." We too were nearing port, cutting by the ambiguous coast. All you see is greenery broken by roofs, but you sense the extraordinary. You have heard amazing stories; you look at the place where they happen.

"Just as the boat sighted dock," I went on, "disaster struck. The ferry lurched, struck bottom, and sank. Everyone drowned!"

"No," said Little Kiwi. "Wait—"

"Ridiculous," cried Dennis Savage. "The bay is four feet deep."

"It sank. Yes. Horrible and true. They held no party that night."

"No *party!*" Little Kiwi repeated, with a miserable groan, as if I had told him that the world's supply of grilled cheese had been exhausted.

"And, so they say, when the moon is full and the Island humming, that ferry rises, a ghost. As midnight strikes, if you approach the harbor, you can hear . . . *the ghastly yapping of a hundred poodles!*"

"*Satirist!*" Dennis Savage hissed, as we pulled in. It was just after lunch. We turned south on the boardwalk to check in with our host, Wacko commenting avidly on the passing scene, and the passing scene, in whispers, commenting avidly on Little Kiwi. About halfway there I looked back and saw that the old man from the bus was following us.

"Maybe he lives in this direction," Dennis Savage said.

"No, he looks guilty. He's *lurking.*" We had stopped, and so had he.

"I'll take care of this," Dennis Savage snapped, starting back.

I grabbed his arm. "Let me talk to him. You're not gentle enough."

"You? You'll throw a drink in his face!"

"That's telling him!" cried Wacko. "Put him in the blender and dial puree!"

Dennis Savage sent the man away, weeping; and Little Kiwi went on snagging hearts. Our host had been having drinks with a friend, who greeted Dennis Savage and me with vacant politesse. But when the friend's eyes lit on Little Kiwi, he turned vivacious. We dropped our luggage at the door and plopped down with dim smiles and nothing to say in the Pines manner. But the man went on and on, addressing himself to Little Kiwi, going for broke. He hung around so long he practically had to be asked to leave. Of course he insisted on kissing us all good-bye. Our host endured it, Dennis Savage made his usual lateral cheek-to-cheek bypass, and I simply picked up some luggage and carried it into a room. But Little Kiwi, the real object of this exercise, wailed, "It's the kiss of death!" and backed away.

I returned to a room made of embarrassment and horror. Apparently this was an Influential Man. Our host turned to me and whispered, "Get him out of here!" through his teeth. I grabbed the man by the collar and was about to swing him toward the door when our host restrained me. "Not him!" he cried. "The *kid!*"

"Come, Little Kiwi, we'll view the ocean."

"He has boils on his nose," Little Kiwi screamed as we left, Bauhaus staggering after us. "He has liver lips!"

"Hush."

"Meet us at tea," Dennis Savage called out at the door. "And do me a favor—lose the puppet."

That part was a cinch: Wacko fell in the water and drowned, and, Bauhaus barking at every wave, Little Kiwi and I walked west along the water's edge. I never know what to say to him, so we moved in silence all the way to the Grove, which Little Kiwi wanted to explore. "This one looks different," he noted—from the Pines, and indeed it is; cramped, campy, and heedless of fashion where the Pines is expansively tense with it. The Grove is like a stomach that has sagged atrociously for twenty years; the Pines is abdominals perfectly turned.

"Why are we here?" Little Kiwi suddenly asked.

"We walked here."

"On Fire Island, I mean. Us three."

"For fun."

"No."

"For adventure."

He shook his head.

"Okay, you tell me."

"No, it was your idea to come out here. What are you two planning?"

I said nothing. We were walking back along the beach, admiring the sunset. The sand was nearly deserted, though here and there solos and small groups were playing out the day's concerto of desire and regret. Ahead of us we saw a tall, dark-haired, very well-built, and extremely handsome man of about thirty-five stalk down the beach toward a young, fair man in the surf up to his thighs. As the older man neared him he turned and they stared at each other for a long moment. Everything else around us seemed to stop, too. The older man very gently stroked the youth's chest. The youth returned the gesture, but not willingly—uneasily, maybe, in a beautiful alarm, never taking his eyes from the man's own. They went on trading these compliments in a kind of reverie, hypnotized by the setting, by their utter disregard for the received inhibitions of Western civilization, and perhaps by their own grandeur as archetypes, like unto like. It was awesome: turbulent and still. So open, so secret. It was the magic of the Island. Oblivious of the rest of us, the two finally stopped touching and just looked. Then the man put his arm around the boy's shoulders and together they walked out of the water and across the sand to the boardwalk.

Little Kiwi looked at me. "Do they know each other?"

"I don't believe so."

"They just . . . met? Like that?"

"It happens."

"Is it going to happen to me?"

"Do you want it to?"

He was silent. Then: "What is it *for?*"

"What's an orange for? Or shoes?"

"I *ate* an orange," he replied. "I *wore* a shoe."

We reflected, looking out upon the sea. Bauhaus, whose existence is an endless chain of wrong choices, rushed sneezing out of the surf, wrestled frantically in the sand, gobbled seaweed, and threw up.

"That dog of yours," I said, "is going to make a big hit at tea."

58

We arrived late and put in the worst sort of entrance: moodily pensive. Dennis Savage's eyes narrowed as we joined him. Our host was high, however, and forgave me five or six times for our faux pas with the Influential Man. "Well, he really is a troll," our host admitted. "He has everything but the bridge. Dear me, that little boy has a nice frown. Where did Dennis Savage find him, do you suppose?"

We gazed dotingly upon Little Kiwi. A huge weightlifter in silk pajama bottoms also took note of him, moved near, and smiled down like a rainbow as Little Kiwi slowly looked up at him.

"You're the sweetest little thing on the Island," said the weightlifter, "and that's a fact." He ran a finger down the front of Little Kiwi's shirt and hooked it on his belt, pulling him closer. "Think we could arrange something, babe?"

Little Kiwi dropped his eyes; his fingers rustled as if Wacko the Puppet were turning over in his grave. Then he looked at the man and said, "Little Kiwi is afraid of you."

The weightlifter laughed, patted Little Kiwi's head, and moved off as Dennis Savage glared daggers in my direction.

"Don't look at me," I told him. "I'm not in this scene."

Oh yes, I was. As our host and Little Kiwi collaborated on dinner in the kitchen, Dennis Savage laid me out to filth in the living room.

"What have you done to him? What did you say? Where did you take him? I've never seen him like this before. He's . . . *crestfallen.*"

"He saw the magic of the Island."

"I'll just bet he did! When he left this house today he was a Pan of the Circuit. He had presto, mistos, contempo."

"Sounds like a new series of designer bank checks."

"This always happens when I let him alone with you!" Dennis Savage raged. "That time I had flu and he had dinner at your place, he came back saying the world was going to end. He was afraid of the dark for weeks!"

"He asked about Spengler's theories because he saw—"

"Spengler! *Spengler?* Little Kiwi wouldn't know Spengler if he caught him rimming Hegel in Xenon!"

"The book happened to be lying open on the ottoman of my armchair and he asked me—"

"I suppose you and he discussed Kant this afternoon and that's why he showed up at tea in such a merry mood!"

"Oh, Christ! What should I have done, then—taken him to the meat rack? What do you think the magic of the Island is, pray?"

"It's ever such delicious quiche, of course!" cried our host, sweeping in with a hot one. "And salad! *Vino!*" Trivets and flatware erupted and settled. "Now, get set for, yes, the *pêche de résistance!* Okay, Little Kiwi!"

Out came Little Kiwi, solemnly bearing a bowl of fruit.

"Look," declaimed our host, "at what Little Kiwi made!"

"Grapes and a peach?" I asked.

"He made *fruit selection!*"

"By myself," Little Kiwi added.

We tried to make dinner festive, but Little Kiwi's funk seemed to have deepened. Every innocent gambit of conversation I played somehow kept coming around to Heavy Topic, Dennis Savage could utter nothing but insults (directed at me), and our host became so dizzy trying to enliven us that the table might have been flying through the air at a drag ball. Even Bauhaus picked up on our troubles; he was whining so, we had to tie him up out on the deck. Finally, in desperation, we tried eating in silence, whereupon poor Little Kiwi put his head down and wept.

We were too shocked to do anything. Or no: we did that stupid, helpless, wasteful thing—we sat and watched.

"I don't want to," Little Kiwi told us. "I don't like it."

Our host started to get up, but Dennis Savage signaled him not to. "What don't you want?" Dennis Savage asked evenly.

"I don't know what to call it." Little Kiwi wiped his eyes but they just got wet again.

"You know what it might be?" our host suggested. He lives quietly, has never had a lover, and isn't used to Scenes. (I could visualize him asking, like Little Kiwi, "What are they *for?*") "We raced home from tea-dancing and went right into the kitchen, so we never took that wonderful Fire Island time out on the deck to sip a cocktail and watch the sun go down."

"That isn't it," I told him.

"Don't be too sure," he replied. Little Kiwi was still crying, head down, grabbing the sides of his chair, a sweet doubting no with hurt feelings and soft black hair. "Almost all my guests tell me how much they love just sitting out there in that silence with their friends. I would read Walt Whitman aloud to them, but I don't dare, of course. Still, the atmosphere is so . . . well, so magical that—"

"Look," I said, "I'll tell you about the magic of the—"

"Little Kiwi," said Dennis Savage dangerously. "Stop crying."

"Oh dear," said our host, "you don't think it was the quiche, do you?"

"And this," Dennis Savage went on, eyeing us two like Monstro the Whale, "is not the time to discuss the magic of the Island. *Do you mind?*"

Clearly it was time to leave them alone, though I must say our host handled it more suavely than I. "I love to go walking on the beach at night," he began; I just grabbed a pear from the fruit selection and shouted "Amscray time!"

We took Bauhaus with us, and traipsed along the water's edge dishing the day's events. I told him about the two men we had seen making magic in the water and he laughed sadly. "Love in the fast lane, isn't it?" he said. "You know, when the three of you arrived, I thought that little boy was a hustler."

"Little Kiwi? Good grief, he's from Cleveland or something."

"Hustlers come from Cleveland."

"Hustlers come from Queens."

"Hustlers come *in* queens."

Another of those elegant nights in the Pines.

Dennis Savage caught up with us after a bit, his cool recovered. As to what had troubled Little Kiwi, he would say nothing other than that the storm was over and the boy had gone to bed. Now it was time for the Lord Mayor of the Circuit to touch base with his cohorts. Our host begged to go along and I proposed to take Bauhaus home and make my fortieth attempt at *Middlemarch*.

"Aye, ever improving himself," said Dennis Savage as we started back. "How inspiring the variety of life in the Pines. Some to their books . . . others to hold court."

"And still others to make a pilgrimage," I added, "slinking through the trees toward love."

"That," replied Dennis Savage, "is your gay materialism speaking. It will be the ruin of you yet."

If there's a lightbulb in all of the Pines bigger than ten watts I've yet to see it. One comes here to be in stories, not read them. Holding *Middlemarch* about three inches from my nose, I had the sensation I was back in the days of the Inquisition, reading forbidden text by secret light. I gave it up, fixed myself a triple Scotch, and went out on the deck to listen to the ocean. There Little Kiwi joined me in running shorts and Dennis Savage's old Hamilton College sweatshirt.

"I'm still embarrassed," he said after quite some wait.

"Dennis Savage went visiting with our host."

He sighed. "I guess I'll have to try to be older, won't I?"

"Now, that's a Fire Island first. Everyone else here is trying to renovate."

"I could have a secret dream and become. Like those party guests on the ferry that sank."

"What would you become, do you think?"

"Virgil Brown."

"Say what?"

He sat on the bench along the deck railing, facing the ocean. "Could I have a sip of your drink?" He tried it and shuddered. "I don't like liquor. I like the sound of the ocean, though."

"It's restful, isn't it?"

"That's my name: Virgil Brown. You can call me that, if you like. Virgil Brown. Mister Brown. That Brown man. You know."

"Okay."

"Do you think Dennis Savage will call me that?"

"He will if you ask him to."

We watched Bauhaus ooch along the deck planks on his stomach, growling.

"I like to listen to the waves," he went on. "I've been to beaches before but I've never heard them sound like this." Bauhaus whimpered and drooled. "Is our host sore at me?"

"On the contrary, I imagine he found it all very stimulating."

"He thought it was the quiche." Little Kiwi laughed very gently. "That was so . . . nice . . . of him. Wasn't it?" Bauhaus rolled over on his back and posed with his legs in the air, a big dead roach.

"Are you cold?" I asked him. "I brought an extra sweater. It's in my satchel."

"Could I sit on your lap and put my arms around you?"

"Of course."

"Grownups do this sometimes," he said, settling in. "It isn't only for kids."

We listened to the ocean pound out its rhythm in the great empty dark of the place where all men are forms of lover because they hunger so, the gayest place on earth, all ours.

"This is the magic of the Island," he said. He lay his head on my shoulder and closed his eyes, listening.

Three Infatuations

All gay is divided into three parts: looks, money, and wit, in that (descending) order, and my friend Carson had some of each—decent looks, tons of money, and competent wit. He'd get by. Perhaps he expected too much. He was always *casing* men—not cruising them as much as considering how they might figure in his plot. Let a waiter come to our table happy with menus, or a truck driver ask the time, or an actor cross a stage, and Carson would be wondering what he would be like to live with. Later, he would ask you where you thought the waiter went, or whom the trucker knew, or what the actor thought.

"I could buy all the men in the world, I expect," he told me. "I could rent the Colt stable, one after the other, night of my nights. But *then* what happens? What is life without mystery?"

Let the rest of us buddy up with persons very much like ourselves, clone for clone; not Carson. He craved the ad, the rendezvous by graffito, the remote, posed photo. Yet all his archetypes ordered out of the catalogue kept turning into real people. There was the weightlifter Carson met in his gym, an agreeable, speechless hunk who fascinated Carson till the night he returned early from a family trip to find the weightlifter dancing around the room in a picture hat to Carol Channing records. Or there was the swimming champ from Rutgers who used to wake up screaming from unspeakable dreams (but he spoke of them); or the vocal coach with the wonderful beard who suffered temporary impotence every time he heard

64

Leonie Rysanek mentioned. There was another weightlifter, a German who knew no English and was turning out great till Carson took him to Fire Island and he went crazy at the quality of the competition and wrecked the house they were staying in.

My favorite was Kurt, a trim dark kid Carson picked up on Christopher Street and took—and kept—home. Carson's term for Kurt's type, for reasons that I'm glad to say were kept obscure, was "sweet gypsy butt." Yet, overnight, Kurt turned into what is generally termed a wife. Carson said Kurt was incredible in the lay, but, underneath Kurt's "I will do anything and I'll do it better than anyone and what's more I'll scream while we're doing it" façade, this kid was against (1) good food, (2) whizz entertainment, (3) hot dancing, and, generally, (4) life. Carson had a tendency to stomach, so Kurt put him on a diet of what looked like hay, and went on to institute farm yard bedtimes and reveilles and refused to go anywhere that held more than eight people.

The night Kern Loften turned forty he threw a stupendous party, and Carson somehow sneaked away from Kurt, arrived early, and dug into his first real food in months. He ate like the Cowardly Lion, ravenously but with a fearful eye over his shoulder watching for Kurt. Remember, this was a kept boy, living with Carson rent-free, board taken care of, pocket money discreetly supplied. And listen to how he carried on with his master:

"What's that in your mouth?" he cried, suddenly upon us and eyes blazing.

"Carrots," said Carson, shooting cookie crumbs all over the place.

"What do you have behind your back?"

"The wall," I whispered.

"You've got pastries and tarts there, haven't you?"

"No," Carson replied. "Celery sticks!"

"Why are they hiding from me?"

"They're afraid you'll gobble them up," I told him. "They want to live."

Kurt regarded me balefully. "I know about you," he said—he always said this when one of Carson's friends picked on him. God, was he cute; but what a bore. "We're leaving *right* now!" he told Carson.

"*You're* leaving. In many ways." And he took his arm from behind him to reveal a bowl of M&Ms. We cheered as Kurt stormed out.

"Well," Carson remarked. "That's the end of him, isn't it?" He meant it, too. When Carson froze on you—he did so, at times, on a whim—he stayed frozen. "Here we go again with the locksmith."

"Poor Kurt," said someone.

"They always have somewhere to go," Carson noted. "With the usual check."

We made a night of it, repairing to Carson's apartment for dish therapy and silly acts. Carson celebrated his freedom in the kitchen, heaving out Kurt's pita bread and bran. "Thank God," he screamed, "I'll never have to eat another dish of tofu!"

In the living room, he surveyed us gloomily. "On the other hand, here I am again: rich, young, and reasonably pretty with no one to pet me. What's the use of money if it can't buy love?"

We wondered.

"I've tried all the kinds, haven't I?" he went on. "Man dudes, sweet gypsy butt, disco league"—here Kurt slammed in, eyed us with ire, and marched off to his last night in the local bed, as Carson wryly ignored the whole thing. "I even had a preppy once. The summer," he sighed, "of '74. So now what?"

It was time for Dennis Savage to theorize. "You've been buying the wrong kind of love," said he. "You haven't had hustlers; you've had gays who charged money. You need a real hustler, who knows his trade and works at it."

Sensation in the room.

"What *is* a real hustler?" someone asked.

"That's a good gay question," says Dennis Savage. "What does a hustler have, besides expert love technique?"

"A hustler doesn't have anything," I offered. "A hustler lacks."

"Yes!" Carson cried. "Yes!"

"All your protégés had things—hang-ups, rules, plans. A hustler is the essence of the thing, a poster made flesh."

"What *doesn't* a hustler have, exactly?" asked Dennis Savage.

"No background?" Carson suggested.

"No mind," someone put in.

"No ambition," said another.

"No interests!" said Dennis Savage, hoping to cap it. But I love to flunk him:

"A hustler," I announced climactically, "has no opinions."

There was silence; then Carson leaped up ecstatically. "Where do I find someone like that?"

As we know, I live on Fifty-third Street between Third and Second, Hustler Alley, and it was there, of course, that Carson would find one, if one could be found. I had doubts. The hustler, after all, is a platonic essence, and real-life humans are less concisely derived.

"I'm auditioning," Carson blithely told me when we bumped into each other one summer evening, I with a bag of groceries and he with about nineteen eyes, all going at once, up street and down, to right and left, quick shots, double takes, and pans, swiveling to follow. It's standard but it's rude.

"Aren't you afraid you'll catch something?" I asked him.

"I'm not actually doing them yet. We're still in the interview stage. To screen out the ones with opinions."

He winked and moved on; I'd never seen him so urbane. But then spending power tends to emphasize the suave in the wealthy.

I took to having the evening cocktail with Dennis Savage. His apartment, two floors above mine, fronts on Fifty-third, so we could sit at the window and watch Carson's auditions. Actually, he seldom materialized. I gather he spent most of his time in the neighborhood's several hustler bars. But we did see quite some parade: the most spectacular boys alongside the most atrocious, the latter as confident or druggy or disturbed as the former; hunks and skeletons; outfits and rags; slick buyers in vested suits and hopeless browsers with damp polyester underarms. You'd think the stage had but two character types, the beauty and the beast, and one topic, their encounter. But every viewing brought new themes, startling variations.

"Is it a microcosm?" I asked, playfully.

"No," says Dennis Savage. "No, it has no texture. Here you see gay reduced to one element: porn. It will be amusing to see what Carson comes up with. Will he find the male who is made of nothing but sex? Think of it: an unconflicted gay!"

We thought of it.

"However," he added, "I've never known Carson to finish anything he started *and* it takes him years not to do it. If he were the captain of the *Titanic* it would still be sinking."

But Carson came through on this one. Jimmy was about twenty-four, tall, and handsome, with straight sandy hair, a roguish smile, hot slit eyes, and a classic kid's frame opulently fleshed out. He had none of the gay things—no quickness, no points of reference, no curiosity. I doubted he had ever seen the inside of a gym or a cabaret. He was amiable and quiet. Carson had us all over for drinks, one by one, to show him off, to get him used to us, and to acclimatize him to gay society. And of course, like those characters in *The Wizard of Oz,* we all compared notes to learn if we had each met the same god. Oz, a figure entirely made of fantasy, appeared differently to each beholder; but Jimmy, no matter who saw him, was one thing: a lost boy.

At Carson's urging, Jimmy told us stories about his adventures, our coterie ranged around him, a Central Committee on gay style, as Carson wandered in and out with *table d'hôte*. It sounds stiff, but I remember being spellbound. Jimmy had actually grown up in an orphanage, run away, held a thousand jobs, and lost them for reasons he never understood. (I could have told him: a boy this beautiful has to keep moving—at liberty, he could blow a community apart.) I saw, as he spoke, that I had misconceived what a hustler is. He doesn't lack opinions—he lacks psychology. Jimmy knew nothing of human interaction. He couldn't read a face or gauge vocal tone, couldn't extrapolate vibe, could scarcely tell you what someone looked like.

And what ghastly tales he shared. From anyone else, these stories would have been ace dish. After hearing them from Jimmy, I wanted to run into a church and shiver. Once he told us about a bordello he worked in Dallas, where the boys were never allowed to leave. The place was run by a huge fat slob and discipline enforced by a nameless hunk covered with tattoos.

"He had no name?" Dennis Savage asked. "None at all? What did you call him?"

"I never said anything to him."

"No, how did you refer to him when he wasn't around?"

"We called him The Man."

"Tell them what you called the fat guy," Carson put in. "Sheila."

We laughed; Jimmy didn't. He was like a TV news reporter reading text, each story a meaningless announcement. He told us that when one of the bordello boys tried to escape, as deterrent punishment The Man would strip the culprit, paddle his butt, then roughfuck him.

We were scandalized; and somewhat aroused. "*Roughfuck* him?" cried one of us. "Fan me with a tulip, mother!" cried another. "What on earth," I asked, "is roughfucking?"

Jimmy looked at Carson, got a nod, and said, "That's when the top man lays you face down on your junk, and after he starts to punk you he turns you on your side and locks his arms around you so you can't pull away. Then he finishes you

69

off by pumping as deep and hard as he can. It hurts a lot after your ass has been paddled."

Of course we wanted more details. We have read Mann, Joyce, Proust. We are the cream of the cultural capital and we want the *eyes* of the story. "Was he ruthless?" we asked. "The Man? Did he get off on hurting you? Would he comfort you afterward?"

Jimmy thought. "No. He just . . . he came in and did it and then he went away somewhere."

"Your junk," we were murmuring in a daze. "What's the other side called?" and when Jimmy answered, "Your candy," we weren't sure what move to make. Then he added, "The Man called it your honeycomb—because it's so sweet to rim, I guess," and we became quite riotous.

Walking home, Dennis Savage and I marveled at this noble primitive brought among us.

"I wonder," said Dennis Savage, "if I should try rough-fucking Little Kiwi."

"Oh, for heaven's sake!"

"On the other hand, I wouldn't know where to buy a paddle."

"Carson," I said once when we were alone, "can this story be true?"

Carson beamed. "He's the real thing, my boy. Just keep encouraging him the way you do, you and the old gang. I've got to get him into shape for the gay life, don't I?"

"Do you?"

"These are just the tryouts. When he's ready, I'll take him out for his debut." I must have had an odd look on my face, for he patted my shoulder and said, "No, don't worry, my old. He picks things up very easily. And he looks *marvelous* in a sweater."

Carson had us over for dinners and Jimmy was the conversation piece, fascinating as such. We had had our fill of collegiate dazzle, show biz dazzle, and porn star dazzle; proletarian dazzle was a novelty. It was like meeting Wild Bill

70

Hickok after a decade of Guy Madison. Paradoxically, Jimmy did look marvelous in a sweater. And he was picking things up, as Carson said. He had the ability to *listen* that makes genuine charm. He was learning the nouns and terms. He never read, but he took to fine music and was wild for film. By the time the opera season was in swing, barely three months after he had moved in with Carson, Jimmy had seen more Ingmar Bergman than I had logged in ten years. It was at the opera that I met them, in fact, the two superb in pinstriped vested suits with identical grins heading toward me on the Grand Tier promenade.

"Isn't he something?" Carson asked me of Jimmy. "He outclasses half the people I know." And Jimmy looked around us to see if it was true.

It was. Gays were spraying the Met with bitter *mots* and anguished looks, their input and output alike a distilled putdown, while Jimmy could shake your hand, hold your eye, and ask about the things he remembered you liked. Others went through motions; Jimmy, because he had to learn them and was warned that they mattered, legitimized them.

"Everyone's looking at you," I told them. "You couldn't attract more attention in this place if you were Leonard Bernstein and Franco Zeffirelli. I can feel the eyes on my back."

"Leonard Bernstein conducts my record of Beethoven's Fifth," said Jimmy, in a tone you might use for "Leonard Bernstein eats asparagus tips" or "Leonard Bernstein roughfucks Sylvia Sass when he's in Budapest."

No opinion, still. But he was smiling now, often. There cannot have been a nicer hustler in New York; Carson's friends would call up when Carson couldn't possibly have been in just to hear Jimmy's voice. I wondered if anyone of the gang fantasized slipping into Carson's shoes, or perhaps assuming Jimmy's contract when Carson finished with him. Of course, without Carson's amazing apartment and amazing bank account and amazing social calendar, a Jimmy might seem questionable. And was there not, in some minds, a sense of failure attached to the taking of a lover on salary—

though we know that half the romances in the Great World are predicated on the doing of a deal?

Everyone hungers, but who *loves?* I wondered, when Carson took me to lunch for my birthday and spent most of it picking the absent Jimmy to pieces. I was thinking of the subculture's great love stories. Did a single one of them involve a hustler? You can be destroyed, as Mac was; or amused, as Carson is. But loved?

"He asks too many questions," Carson was saying. "Why doesn't he quit while he's ahead?"

"Stop complaining, Carson. You've got the hottest partner in the seventeenth precinct."

"Oh, I admit his sense of devotion is touching. And he does have the most spectacular nipples on the east coast, big as half-dollars. Yes. True. Yes." He sighed. "I just wish he'd stop . . . what do I wish?"

"I wish you appreciated what a neat couple you make."

"I wish you knew what it's like working the Circuit with a god in tow. Everyone comes running up to ask *Who is that one?* in that breathless way." He imitated: *"Who, Carson, tell? It's sizeable, isn't it? What's his service? What's his code name? Does it talk?* How would you like to live with that?"

"His code name is The Man."

"You know what he calls the stereo? The 'record machine'!" He made a face. "I wonder if I suffer from sex nausea. Like Shakespeare in the late romances."

"Your trouble is, you can't accept good fortune."

"It's sizeable, isn't it?" He snorted.

It lasted through April, and ended sweetly, calmly, and sadly. This was Jimmy's doing, those his qualities—Carson always liked to go out fighting. He told it far and wide how he threw Jimmy out, and no one believed him. The likes of Carson seldom make it into a room with a Jimmy, let alone dismiss him. But I know it was Carson who pulled the cord, because Jimmy came over to my place when he left on his way to the rest of his life. Everything was wool and cotton; the

72

boy had been done over so completely you might have glimpsed him in *GQ*. Yet he retained his honest incomprehension of the patterns by which we enact ourselves—so well that if he were to appear on a soap opera his artlessness would shatter the great American television screen.

"I have to talk," he said as he set down his suitcases. "And I don't know what to say."

"We need a drink."

"Scotch, neat. A twist if you have one."

You churl, I told myself in the kitchen, because I was thinking I knew him when he couldn't have named a brand of beer. Not surprisingly, he had had no trouble securing a place to move to; he was already set, in fact. I couldn't identify the name he gave me, but I could visualize the scene: more money than Carson, less to do, and atrocious friends. Love seats, plane trips, and cast parties. East Seventies stuff. Was this the step up or down?

We talked. "There's only one thing I can do," he told me. "I tried to be so hot in bed that he would never let me go. And I know I'm good. I know I am. I spoke to him, you know, giving the choices. There's pimp style, little-boy style, party style . . ."

And roughfuck, I thought, trying and failing to see Carson getting paddled. Junk side down, I thought. Flip over on your candy, I thought. Should I offer him my money and my life?

". . . if someone would pick me out of the crowd like that and . . . well, keep me. I used to wonder about it. You know? Imagine it? How he would look and the things he'd say to me." He grinned, sadly. "He wasn't anything like Carson."

I told him that we all fantasize.

"I admire him," he said.

I told him that Carson was beyond admiration, or too far before it.

"He isn't easy to get along with. But I'm going to miss him. I'll miss all of you. This was a wonderful year. It was the first thing I've ever belonged to."

73

I didn't tell him that the only thing he had ever truly belonged to, because gay is the most class-conscious of cultures, was Sheila's bordello. Because opinions are what define us. Because, despite our best intentions, Jimmy was all candy and all junk. Hell, most of the people I know divide you in half if you didn't go to Yale, Chicago, Penn, or Swarthmore. *I tried to make myself so hot in bed.* Who doesn't? I told him, "You're a gay Galatea."

He waited for the explanation, as he always did, antennae quivering. "Pygmalion sculpted Galatea, *created* her. Then he fell in love with her."

Jimmy nodded. "Only this time he didn't."

"Next time," I said. "In fact, I was going to suggest—"

Suddenly he blurted out, "Why do I like him? Why? He was so cruel . . . last night he said . . . he said . . ."

"Because we get crushes on the men who teach us to be wonderful."

And in crashed Dennis Savage and Little Kiwi, at least without Little Kiwi's endlessly horrendous dog Bauhaus. The commotion eased the atmosphere, and Jimmy took his leave, clapping us all on the shoulder and swearing to stay in touch. Little Kiwi, who had had limited exposure to this son of sex— father, should I say?—stared at Jimmy and, at the last minute, impetuously rushed forward to throw his arms around him. Jimmy rubbed his back and kept saying "Okay, okay, okay." Little Kiwi backed away as red as some people's underwear, Dennis Savage and Jimmy shared a grave look, and off went the hustler with his suitcases.

That should be the end, Jimmy vanishing into the cashmere despair of the service routes. "He came in, he did it, then he went away somewhere." But, some years later, as I walked up the aisle after *Evita,* a strong hand gripped my arm and I turned and there he was, the pair of us too stunned to speak. He was with a grisly moneygay group, one very tall haughty queen in a fur shako especially regrettable.

"Jimmy," he sizzled, "if you would *detach* yourthelf. We have to get to Roddy and Roberto'th thoiree."

Gosh, I thought, somebody still lisps. Jimmy held on to me, whispering as if he were passing contraband.

"Do you see Carson?"

"Yes, of course. He—"

"Would you please tell him something for me? Something important?"

"Surely, but why don't you—"

"Get out of it, you Tribeca queen!" screamed the haughty shako. "Somebody puth him *away!*"

I reached up and dislodged his hat, and he would have charged and queened me to death but for the crowds pouring past us.

"Look," I said to Jimmy, "why don't you call him yourself? Or you could even drop in on him. Messengers aren't all that effective outside of Sophocles."

He shook his head. "You don't understand."

"Leave these dreadful people," I told him. "Come home with me, and we'll call Carson, or even—"

"Jimmy, please." It was another of the Roddy-Roberto set. "Hugh is having a fit. You'll blow the whole deal if you don't come now."

Jimmy clasped my hand, said, "I remember all of you," and left. And I stood there thinking, Why *Tribeca?* This sweater is from Bloomingdale's.

Naturally, Dennis Savage scoffed when I told him. "That old dish!" he cried. "Half the guys in town don't even know who Jimmy is! And look at you waving an *Evita* playbill at me, you *follower!*"

"Oh, Christ."

"How many times must I tell you? Gays *create* sell-outs; they don't attend them."

"I come to you with the last paragraph of a romantic tragedy and you lecture me on hip!"

"All right," he said. "You met a devastato at the theatre

and he asked you to take a message to friend Carson. Now for dessert: *What* did he want you to tell him?"

"Just for that, I'm not saying."

"I'll guess: 'Carson, please take me back for you are the love of my life.' Right?"

I said nothing. He remembers all of us.

"Or, rather," he went on, "that's what you *hope* the message is, don't you? The name is love. And that is so bizarre, and so inane, and so likable, that it could almost be true. I've always said gay needs more romanticism. You may hawk antique dish and attend old shows, but emotionally you're in the vanguard." He went over to the window and gazed down on Fifty-third Street, upon the parade of the bribed and deluded. "The name is love," he repeated. "The name of a thing is strategic. And there are three names in gay: your own, the name of your one true best friend, and the name of your imaginary lover, whom you never meet."

I joined him at the window. "I can cite one person who met him."

Dennis Savage smiled, utterly misconstruing the allusion. *Three* infatuations, I say. "Who but you," he asked, "would get sentimental over the story of a hustler who developed an opinion? I believe you wear those dark glasses so we can't see you weeping at the pathos of a loveless world."

"*Never!*"

"Look! Down there. Look at them all, the strangers! As if callous, impenetrable beauty were more attractive than feeling intimacy. As if no one dared face himself. I tell you, all gays are liars."

"I haven't wept since I was a child!"

"And that," he said, "is the most stupid lie of all."

The Case of
the Dangerous Man

I hate to give Dennis Savage credit for anything—he'd only get pompous—but his concept of the Imaginary Lover is all-basic to gay culture. It is everyone's direst secret. Few men will as much as breathe his imaginary name to their best friend, much less provide a physical description or character sketch. "This," as Mac McNally once said, "I must not share."

Yet one notes references to the Imaginary Lover everywhere. You are conversing to the dim accompaniment of some dreary television show, a nameless hunk appears, and your comrade discreetly stiffens: this is a clue. You are strolling along the street, something elegant strides by, and your companion murmurs, "I want to bear his child": this is annotation. The unique charm of the Imaginary Lover is that he can never lose his appeal as real humans do, invariably, eventually, for he is a fantasy—plausible but a dream. You may spot someone who looks like him, or cracks his jokes, or lives where he ought to live. You even seem to know what it's like to climb his stairs, and press his buzzer. But to run across the man who accommodates your precise measurements of the romantic utopia is unlikely.

This is just as well, I think, for keeping the fantasy fantastical allows everyone to play. In a culture run by the fascism of looks, the Imaginary Lover is a democratic exercise. A beauty knows he might well land something comparable to supreme, even be one. A nice-looking fellow has a shot at it. A homely-but-hot man is ever loveable. And certain *objets trouvés* may win out through force of personality; unthinkable but true, my favorite combination. Below a certain level of appearance, however, a gay man is in big trouble; yet everyone can dream. And, though no one likes to hear about this, I know that the ugliest man in town visualizes himself being fondled, or toughed up, or tucked in by some divo just as easily as the handsomest man can. But why does no one like to hear about this?

Carlo shook his finger at me when I spoke of the matter late one night. And when I went on undeterred, he held his hand over my mouth and said, "I want you to please stop. I don't want to know about morals, or politics, or death, or feelings, or any of the other things that ruin everybody's fun."

"What morals?" I asked.

"Trolls," he said. "Talking about trolls is talking morals. Or politics."

We were confessing our episodes to each other—My First Time in Bed, My Worst Time in Bed, My Sleaziest Pickup (Carlo had about twenty-five possibilities to choose from; I had none), My Most Daring Pickup (mine was my neighbor Alex: after watching him for a year, I held up a sign in my window asking to come over and watch the Oscars). Suddenly it struck me that all over New York gays were exchanging these stories, and the stories were all the same but the storytellers all different. I wondered how it felt to hear smoking-car braggadocio from a troll, and I verbalized it, and Carlo got upset. But why?

"You always want to make a case out of everything," he said.

This is highest offense to Carlo, the paragon of the carefree gay. There are no cases in Carlo's life. Everything just happens; nothing is questioned, challenged, repudiated. Naturally, he is one of those typeless beauties whom everyone craves, dark but smooth, bright but uneducated, solid but slim: nice and hot. Naturally—you've got to be super cute to enjoy a heedless life. Carlo has more best friends than anyone else I know, all former lovers, for if his erotic appeal is considerable, his gift as sympathetic company is overwhelming. Some men don't truly love him until after their affair has ended.

He is perhaps the most "episodic" of my friends in that he would fall hopelessly in crush every year in late fall and fall out again by the following spring. He favored size, age, and the Latin school of charm, and his lovers were so good-natured that they never held it against Carlo when he abandoned them. Except he never did abandon anyone: he simply collected another best friend. And I note that none of them was spectacular, in the Imaginary Lover manner. They were teddy bears, a little coarse but terribly nice, probably fun in bed and even more fun the next morning. They were all alike, yet they had nothing in common; like Carlo, they had not defined themselves in any certain way. After I had known all of them for years, the thing that sprang to mind when they did was not something any one of them had said or done but how large they all felt when I was jammed onto a couch next to them.

And this is possibly because they did, after all, have one thing in common, something Carlo shared with them: they had jobs but no career. They were gym trainers, or hotel orderlies, or movers. Now and again they hustled. They were the kind of people who never receive junk mail or utter beliefs or yearn for something that happens later than next week. They could be amazingly loyal, even valiant. They just didn't subscribe to anything.

Does it matter? I suppose that depends on what set you run with. But I was raised by a couple who urged me to make something notable of myself, and they didn't mean a banker or a doctor. The world is full of these; artists are ever few. So they sat rapt before my puppet shows (though they were always Punch–and–Judy *guignol* in which all my brothers were murdered), and gave me piano lessons, and took me to Broadway. And when it was all over I was a little crazy and very smart, and I was bound to regard cool Carlo and his unsophisticated lovers with befuddlement. They lacked a theme. Or I would come back from the Eagle having approached someone because of his charm and deserted him because he was professionally unmotivated, and Dennis Savage would chide me, one of his most enthusiastic activities. "Stop making judgments," he once said, "and consult Chatty Cock."

Well, you know, we have these little talks, and, much as I would enjoy kicking his bum in, he is the dearest thing I own. So I say, "Who is Chatty Cock?"

"Chatty Cock," he replies, "is the spirit of the Circuit. He has perfect instincts. He knows what to wear, whom to go with, whether to prevaricate or denude himself—"

"I'll bet a piaster on that."

"—because he doesn't agonize over bourgeois ethics. He doesn't weigh the advantages, as you do. He doesn't try to comprehend the Circuit. Life is short. Consult Chatty Cock and let a thing happen. You need spontaneity."

"You need a muzzle."

"When things get tough, you might assume a restorative posture of comic resistance, reducing the Circuit to a vanity." Dennis Savage doesn't merely theorize; he dictates a proposal to Yale University Press. This is what comes of letting your children attend small, elite men's colleges with pungent English departments, like Hamilton, instead of Sensible Preppy Places like Duke. "When comedy is called for, you might turn to Satyricock." I swear I heard him pronounce the *y*. "Satyricock doesn't get much, I admit, but he's popular and famous."

"I visualize President Taft."

"He's not dear to look at, but he has balance. He'll never figure in disreputable dish, as someone I know so often does."

"What if I don't believe in comic resistance? What if I take everything seriously, including the question of a person's vocation? What if I want my associates to *stand* for something? What about ideas?"

"Then you're in the grip of Murder Cock, and no good can come of it."

"Murder Cock? *He* sounds like the boy to follow."

80

Dennis Savage shakes his head. "See, with Chatty Cock, everything is casual narcissism: do I want to or don't I? With Satyricock, everything is burlesque. Note the choices?"

"And with Murder Cock?"

"With Murder Cock, everything is resistance and counterattack, death and debris. Follow him and no one will like you anymore."

I must admit, he remarks something there—you can have love, war, or nothing. But the trouble with Circuit Theory is the Circuit doesn't observe it. The Circuit is inconsistent, volatile, pandemic.

"Why don't you be like Carlo?" Dennis Savage goes on. "Carlo is Chatty Cock personified."

"Men are what they do," I grumble.

"Not Carlo."

"My point exactly. Carlo doesn't do anything."

"Carlo is a lover," he replies. "That's his calling."

Surely it was; some calling. And what happens when the ace handler of teddy bears runs into a grizzly—better, when the eternal amateur hooks up with a man who does something? This episode is about the marriage of Chatty Cock and Murder Cock.

Carlo would launch his affairs by taking his latest beau around for coffee and commentary, and this year the event fell on My Usual Evening With Dennis Savage.

At my knock, Little Kiwi opened the door a crack, studied me through a magnifying glass, and said, "I detect a literary man."

"I detect a little crumbun," I replied, "who'd better—"

"Little Kiwi!" Dennis Savage cried from behind the door. "I told you to—"

"Inspector Wilberforce," Little Kiwi corrected, as I passed inside. "The Supreme Detective."

"They're not here yet," Dennis Savage told me. "But soon. Autumn doesn't really get going till Carlo pairs off in his annual rite."

"Plus the intrepid canine wonder," Little Kiwi went on, "who has a mystic alias never yet revealed." This, of course, would be Bauhaus, Little Kiwi's phenomenally D-list dog, just then cheezing up under the sofa.

"Oh no," said Little Kiwi. "He ate Oysterettes again."

"Well, who *gave* him Oysterettes?" When he gets tired of palling around with me, Dennis Savage can get a job as a young George Burns in some vaudeville act.

"He eats the box, too," said Little Kiwi, examining my belt buckle through his glass.

"If someone I know doesn't leave off detecting the guests," said Dennis Savage, "he's going to get the spanking of his life tonight."

"Oh, you always say that," said Little Kiwi. "And then nothing happens."

Something did happen: Carlo's new lover, Daniel Johnson, came in. I think the word for him would be "stalwart." He looked like the hero of a western, and moved like one, and sounded like one. Even Carlo seemed awed, and the rest of us were notably subdued, for us. Inspector Wilberforce quite neglected to introduce the canine wonder.

Daniel Johnson was not shy, and he appeared to be observing us keenly. No doubt Carlo had told him something of us, and now he was matching the tales to the subjects. What had he heard? Did Carlo mention the time Little Kiwi blundered through an arcane door, found himself locked in a strange hallway, and disrupted Bloomingdale's housewares department trying to get back into the store? Or the time Dennis Savage and I followed Kern Loften around at a party for hours waiting for him to sit down because we wanted to put an egg under him just before he landed? Mild tales, I know. But they're ours, all the same. Our secrets. Daniel had us at several disadvantages: one, he knew our dish while we didn't know his; two, as the honored guest he commanded our courtesies; and three, he was to die. And he knew it; but he seemed not to care, which is a new one in my catalogue of the Gay Mentalities. I've checked off archetypes who luxuri-

82

ated in their distinction and archetypes who suffered it, but never one who behaved as though there were some eight or nine things that mattered more. And, to judge by the tone of his conversation, morals, politics, death, and feelings were clearly on the list.

Carlo was in bliss, as always at this time of his year, so he was missing a lot. But I noticed that Daniel responded to my mention of *Vile Bodies* not with some bawdy slogan but with a reference to Waugh, and that he nodded in affirmation when I suggested that if Cyrus Vance had been one of the hostages in Iran, the whole crowd would have been freed the first night, and, for that matter, that no one tried to call him Dan or Danny. This was a very self-possessed man.

"Is it permitted to ask how you two met?" Dennis Savage asked.

Carlo grinned.

"I picked him up on the street," said Daniel. "It's not something I normally do. But I saw him and I wanted him, and I figured maybe he ought to know about it."

"In those words?"

"Just about."

"I have never been so completely picked up in my life," said Carlo. "And I've been picked up by experts."

"Where did this happen," said Little Kiwi, recovered from his shyness and strutting around with his hands behind his back like someone in a tweedy salon thriller of the 1920s, "may I ask?"

"This happened at the corner of Bank Street and Seventh Avenue," Daniel replied, suppressing a smile.

"A likely story!" cried Little Kiwi, whirling around and pointing. "I suppose," he tried to snarl, "there were a hundred witnesses?"

"A nun smiled at us," said Carlo.

"Inspector," I put in, "why don't you show Carlo and Daniel your new sweater?"

"Okay!" Little Kiwi loves a new idea. Racing off, he

paused drastically at the bedroom door. "Don't anybody leave this room."

"Go! Sweater! Put on!"

He vanished.

"*This* takes him shopping," said Dennis Savage, meaning me, "and lets him buy a large."

"He insisted."

Carlo was fastened on Daniel, but Daniel was listening to us, and each time his eyes blinked I felt as if a camera had gone off in his head, freezing us in our sport. This was something new in Carlo's love life for certain; his other beaux never saw anything but Carlo.

"Look!" cried Little Kiwi, in his new sweater.

"It goes back tomorrow," said Dennis Savage.

"No!"

"It's too big for you!"

"It makes me look tough!"

It made him look, actually, like a lollipop wearing a teepee. Sensing sympathy for lost causes in Daniel, Little Kiwi turned to him and said, "What do you think?"

Daniel regarded him for a moment, took him by the waist, and said, "I think you're a very sexy boy."

"No, I didn't," said Little Kiwi, breaking loose. Erotic directness still panics him and even jumbles his syntax. He has a way to go yet. But he is picking up defenses here and there: grabbing his detecting glass, he held it up to Daniel's nose and faced him down till he laughed.

"A likely story," Little Kiwi repeated triumphantly.

"How does it feel having your own detective on the premises?" Carlo asked Dennis Savage.

"Not to mention the writer downstairs?" Dennis Savage replied.

"Or the schoolteacher up," I added. "Though he mentions it seldom."

"And me," said Little Kiwi, "Inspector Wilberforce. Plus the canine wonder with a mystic alias never yet revealed."

"The canine wonder?" said Daniel.

"He's hiding under the couch because he ate too many Oysterettes. Daniel, what do you do?"

Daniel smiled, friendly but firm. "That's a secret."

"It is?"

"Yes."

"From Carlo, too?"

Carlo looked baffled. Of course he hadn't yet thought to ask what Daniel did for toil. A job is an obstacle, something that precludes pleasure, like a dentist appointment or going home at Thanksgiving. You wouldn't ask about it. But who would bother to keep it a secret?

"Why can't you tell me?" Carlo asked Daniel.

"Because I can't."

Carlo said, "All right," but he looked as if he wasn't sure it was.

"What do you think of Daniel now?" was the question of the month, as more and more of him showed. I thought he was generous, because he took us all out to dinner; and appreciative, as long as no one attacked the United States or the flag; and hard-headed, when he ran into anything that unreasonably barred his path. Little Kiwi adored him; Dennis Savage regarded him wryly. "He's too wonderful," he said. "There's got to be a flaw, some terrible hidden thing. No one's that . . ."

"Yes?"

He shrugged.

"No, go on," I urged. "Finish the thought and reveal one of your own bitter doubts. Criticism of wonderful men usually does."

"That strong, I was going to say. Is that so revealing, you human bedpan? And while we're at it, what did you mean when you said I seldom mention teaching?"

"Have you been stewing about that all this time? In fact, you never mention teaching at all."

"No one wants to hear about it."

"Most people talk about their work."

"Fascinating. Shall we call Little Kiwi in to tell us about life in the mail room at BBDO?"

In the succeeding silence, I was thinking that I for one talk ceaselessly about writing, my own and others'; it had never occurred to me that anyone worth talking to wouldn't find it enticing. Writing is the world entire: morals, politics, death, and feelings.

Dennis Savage looked away. Was he thinking that a man of education ought to do better in a lover than a mail room assistant? I was. But then I have seen him, over the years, crying, sick, nude, drunk, and raging in despair, so he has long since given up worrying about what I think. I suppose I resent that; but someone who worries about how you feel can be forgiven a lot.

"You know," I said, as carelessly as I dared, "I wouldn't mind hearing about teaching every now and then."

He took a while to respond. "Everyone has flaws. So no one is perfectly suited to anyone else."

"Is that Chatty Cock's wisdom or yours?"

"My wisdom for today is: Not being able to tell your lover what you do in the daytime is *molto* strange."

Carlo thought so, too, which was even stranger. "What could be so terrible," he worried, "that he can't let me in on it?" As so often, Carlo was living on unemployment insurance and had plenty of time for visiting. Most days, by my six o'clock break, if Carlo wasn't at my place I could go upstairs and find him at Dennis Savage's playing Guess Daniel Johnson's Profession.

"Maybe he's rich," said Little Kiwi, taking out his wallet and admiring, as he continually did that month, his first bank plastic, with a credit limit of something like eight dollars. "He's rich, see, but he wants you to like him for himself. That's what his secret is."

"He can't be rich," said Carlo. "He lives in Brooklyn."

"Maybe he owns a house there."

"Rich people don't own houses in Brooklyn," said Dennis Savage. "Rich people own Brooklyn."

"Have you ever seen where he lives?" Little Kiwi asked Carlo.

"No . . ."

Little Kiwi beamed. "Inspector Wilberforce rides again."

"Maybe he's a hit man," I suggested.

"Never," said Little Kiwi. "He's too nice."

"Hit men can be nice."

"Not," said Carlo, pensively, "to the people they hit."

Dennis Savage looked at him.

I looked at him.

Little Kiwi saw something going on and he looked, too.

"Oh, it's nothing like that," said Carlo. He said it too fervently, so we all leaned in for more.

"It's . . . no. Believe me. I was just thinking aloud. I didn't mean anything."

"You never truly know a man till you know what he does in bed," said Dennis Savage. "You know, Carlo. So tell us and we'll decide."

"It's not what you think," Carlo insisted.

"What do we think?"

"This is too deep. I don't want to talk about it."

"What do we think?" said Little Kiwi, baffled. He turned to Carlo. "Does he hit you? In *bed?*"

"You know him, Carlo," I said. "For good or ill, you know him. And it's for good, right? What difference does it make what he does for a living?"

"I should have known you'd take the fascist's side," said Dennis Savage.

"I'm taking Chatty Cock's side, in fact."

"Does Daniel hit Carlo?" Little Kiwi repeated. "Because he was naughty, or what?"

Carlo, who spent his twenties in San Francisco exploring some of the culture's heaviest scenes, said, "Little Kiwi, someday I will sit you down and tell you about dangerous men."

"Daniel is dangerous?" Little Kiwi asked. "He gave me a piggyback ride on Hudson Street!"

"Inspector," I said, "I think this particular topic is over your head."

"The Case of the Dangerous Man," Little Kiwi murmured, amazed.

"I just want to know what he does," said Carlo. "I just want to know."

"'I must see the Things,'" I quoted. "'I must see the Men.'"

"Who said that?" asked Dennis Savage.

"The crazy part," Carlo went on, "is I left San Francisco to get away from it. Do you know what I like? After all this? Do you know? I like playful men. Playful and affectionate. The trouble with S and M is that it . . . it does something. It's more than sex. It's like an act you would be hired to do in an after-hours club."

"It makes a case out of love," I observed.

Carlo nodded.

"But Daniel *is* playful," said Little Kiwi.

"You know what?" said Carlo. "Daniel is a lot of things."

I feel like something of an inspector myself, as I unravel my tales, making cases of everyone I know. As I write, my neighbor across the way is standing in her window with a male friend, pointing at me. "See?" she says, I guess. "There he is again, watching." Yes, I watch; but not her.

Or yes, sometimes I do, fleetingly. She is very attractive, dresses for power, and constantly changes her clothes: for the office, for dinner, for rendezvous. The man is older than she. When he comes in at night, he wears a lawyer's suit, but peels down to Oz-green jockey shorts. Once I saw him push her onto the bed, and without anything else to go on—the lights immediately went out—I could not tell whether he was being playful or dangerous.

"We are not alone," my friend Eric told me once, as we walked up Third Avenue after dinner. "*Everyone* is mad." Only the truly bizarre is normal in New York, where spiffy men in Lord & Taylor trench coats and bearing haughty at-

88

taché cases walk past you carrying on irate conversations with invisible associates. Then I encounter Little Kiwi at the treats section in Sloan's, looking as wan as Tiny Tim because his favorite flavor of Pop-Tarts—brown sugar–cinnamon—is out of stock. And I think, thank heaven, *someone* is still sane.

We trudge home together past the little kids solemnly pushing their own strollers, and the people with the latest Bloomingdale's bag, and the dreary hustlers attempting industrial-strength come-hither smiles, and Little Kiwi asks me, "Does Daniel really hit Carlo?"

How do you explain S and M to someone who thinks belts grow on pants? "He doesn't hit him, exactly. He . . ." What? "He romanticizes him. He takes him out of the world and engulfs him."

"With what?"

"Concentration."

The doorman hands me a messengered package as we turn into our lobby—page proofs of my latest book.

"What's this one about?" Little Kiwi asks.

"Same as the others. Morals, politics, death, and feelings."

"No wonder you're always grouchy."

Carlo met us at Dennis Savage's door, in the heat of debate. "Isn't it a lover's job," he asked, "to be honest and true?"

"Now what?" I asked Dennis Savage.

"Tell him, Carlo."

Carlo threw himself onto the couch as Little Kiwi and I sat with our brown paper grocery bags on our laps. We looked like steerage passengers awaiting our examination at Ellis Island.

"I found a gun in his room," said Carlo.

"You went to Brooklyn?"

"A gun in a leather holster."

"Instead of in what, a macramé potholder?"

"A gun in a holster in the top drawer of his bureau!"

"What must he have in his closet?"

"I didn't get a chance to check the closet. He went to the bathroom and I just had a—"

"*With gloves?*" cried Little Kiwi. "So you don't leave fingerprints? Carlo, can I come with you next time you snoop around in Brooklyn?"

"A man with a gun!" Carlo pleaded. "Don't you understand? Won't you please listen?"

Bauhaus, feebly barking, pattered in from the bedroom on the way to his water dish as we contemplated Carlo's predicament.

"Tell me what to do," said Carlo.

"Carlo," I explained, "you are one of the most experienced men in American gay. You helped break styles in in San Francisco, Los Angeles, and New York. Factions have formed around you. Bars have mooed in wonder upon your entrance. If James Joyce had known you, Molly Bloom would have been a man. How can anyone tell you what to do in romance?"

Carlo heaved a sigh of profound discontent. "If only I knew what that gun does."

"I'll find out!" cried Little Kiwi. "This is a job for Inspector Wilberforce! With his intrepid canine wonder, whose mystic name . . ."

The canine wonder slunk past us with the biggest dog yummy I've ever seen between his teeth.

"What are those?" I asked. "Elephant biscuits?"

"Little Kiwi," said Dennis Savage, "I don't want that dog eating in the bedroom."

Little Kiwi shrugged. "He likes to dine in utter silence. It's too noisy in here."

"I'm going to break it off with him," said Carlo suddenly. "I mean it."

"Carlo, if you love him—"

"Love is for twinkies."

"*What?*"

"I'm not like you." He looked at us, all of us, and this

time we leaned back and away. "We don't believe the same things."

Silence.

"Don't be sore at me," he went on. "I'm not saying I'm better than you. I just know about other deals. I don't make cases out of everything."

"Deals?" said Dennis Savage. "You think love is a deal?"

"You're making a case out of Daniel Johnson," I observed.

Carlo nodded. "Good for me. Because he's not doing what he's supposed to do. And I *will* drop him, watch."

More silence, penetrated by the sounds of distant teeth breaking up a biscuit.

"I have to go," said Carlo; and he went.

"It isn't the gun," said Dennis Savage, after a moment. "Or the mystery job. And Oscar Wilde knows it's not S and M."

"Then what?" I asked. "Is Daniel too dangerous for Carlo?"

Dennis Savage slowly shook his head. "There's a missing piece somewhere."

"Is it possible," I asked, "that, for the first time, our Chatty Cock has come face to face with Murder Cock?"

"It wouldn't be the first time. Carlo is smarter than he likes to think he is, and he learns by doing. What has he done for fifteen years? He has made love to men. Men is what he knows, all the kinds. Believe me, Murder Cock and Carlo are graduates of the same school. And so is Daniel Johnson."

"So what's the missing piece?"

"I think I know," said Little Kiwi.

Dennis Savage patted the sofa next to him and Little Kiwi dutifully arrived there.

"No," Dennis Savage told him. "You don't know. And if I have any contribution to make, you never will. Okay?"

"For the sake of heuristics, Inspector," I put in, "what do you think the missing piece is?"

"Love."

"How so?"

"I don't think Carlo has ever been in love. You know how I know?"

"How?" asked Dennis Savage, putting an arm around him.

"Because he isn't afraid of anything."

"That may well be," I said. "He has never thought about what it's like. Right? He just does it."

"What's 'it'?" asked Dennis Savage.

"Love . . . no, I mean, a lover—*No,* I mean, the Imaginary Lover. One's concept of what love is supposed to feel like. That's 'it.' And Carlo has no concept. He is his own Imaginary Lover. And you know what I think? I think Daniel wants to be Carlo's Imaginary Lover, and things are getting hot. Very, unbalanced, true-love hot. And Carlo is uncertain. For the first time in his life."

No one said anything for a bit. Then, "If I were Carlo," Little Kiwi observed, "I would be uncertain, too. I might even start being afraid."

After that, there was little for me to do but take my groceries home, sit down at my desk, open the notebook, and distress my neighbor.

Carlo did throw Daniel over, spang in the middle of winter, completely upsetting everybody's schedule. Our friend would be available when he should have been occupied, the droop when he ought to be the hedonist, and chaotically in doubt when he owed us the directness of a pilot. I had not realized before how much a guide Carlo had been, trading his lack of sophistication for our hunger for data on sensuality. We taught him how to bluff his way through brunch; he taught us how to play a bar. If the Circuit is ice, Carlo had slipped; now he was breaking through and would drown. "Tell me what to do," he had said—*Carlo* needed telling!

He certainly didn't need any tutorials in how to drop a lover. He believes catastrophic announcement works best, and drops mates the way gunfighters of the Old West dropped their challengers: he shoots them down in cold blood. As far as I can see, he doesn't give off warning signs of recalcitrance or hostility, or arrive late for dinner, eyes avid after some rebellious tryst, or become inexplicably unavailable. No. It is as if it has suddenly occurred to him that he doesn't want a lover anymore. And he will turn to his innamorato and say, "Would you mind if we didn't see each other for a while?" He's very nice about it, almost gentle, once he detonates his bomb. He just means to announce that he's had enough, thank you, enough.

But every so often we run across someone who doesn't suit our behavior patterns—indeed, one who plans to overwhelm them. For the French, it may be the German army. For writers, it may be your editor's replacement, who ushers you into a third-rate café, smiles engagingly, and says, "There's a problem." For gays, it may be the man who doesn't take no for an answer.

Carlo's no had never been challenged, because, frankly, the man is so good-looking that most other men accept his rejection as their due—the sole instance, I believe, in which gay is inferior to straight. The average heterosexual man, turned down for a dance, a date, or a fling, tends to think the woman had made a foolish mistake. Gays in a comparable position mope or frantically double the weights in their workout. Perhaps Carlo got his first no this time around because Daniel is even better-looking than Carlo; perhaps because Daniel really is dangerous; perhaps because it was high time. Anyway, Daniel did not take no for his answer.

"He's after me," said Carlo, walking into my apartment one afternoon, as you might say, "The grocery clerk overcharged me."

"After you?"

"He won't let me alone. Daniel. He says if I don't talk it out with him he's going to . . ." I was trying to look blasé, but I don't wear dark glasses in the apartment and my eyes gave

93

me away. Carlo stopped; he has no more desire to become Dish of the Week than you or I, boys and girls.

I thought of all those sizeable sweethearts Carlo had acquired—Wayne Hibbard, the only man I've met who cries when his favorites don't win Oscars; or Scooter Smith, so kind-hearted he has had mercy sex with some of the most atrocious men in New York; or Big Steve Bosco, so ebullient that he hugs strangers on the street. Daniel was broader, cooler, and more judgmental than they, and I could easily see him refusing the role of the discard.

"He's tough, isn't he?" I asked, though it wasn't a question.

"Do you know what he did? The night of the Blue Party, we were going back to my place, and at the corner of my block this guy came up at us with a knife."

My face must have been too blank, for Carlo decided to backtrack. "The Blue Party, remember? When Frank Donner came in Arabian pajamas and Eddie Palladino grabbed his—"

"I wasn't there."

"How could you not be there?"

"Probably because my pen was flying and I didn't want to throw away an evening of A-list work just to go to another night of . . ." I trailed off. He doesn't approve and he never will, no matter how I explain it.

"I've been to so many parties," I tell him.

"I know, Bud. But each one—"

"Is not as interesting to me as what I can do at my desk." He shakes a finger at me.

"You and my neighbor should get together," I tell him. "She thinks I should get out more, too."

"Sometimes I don't think I can talk to you anymore."

"A guy with a knife," I prompt.

"Yeah." He nods. "Yeah. And he was whispering. Listen, it was like . . . like 'Some for me, now.' Like that: 'Some for me.'" Carlo paused, shifted position, brooded. I always take my desk chair and leave the big black armchair with the ottoman for the guests, giving me the chance to tower over them in an academic manner, like a psychiatrist. I might lay in a supply of threatening little pads and take up saying, "Any dreams lately?"

"Well, so Daniel did this . . . maneuver, or something. I didn't see it, exactly. Something like karate. Turning and kicking. And the guy went down like . . . like he had never been there. Didn't even scream. And Daniel picked up the guy's knife and said, 'Let's go,' and he took my arm and he kind of . . . pulled me along. About seven doors down the street he threw the knife into a garbage can. And I was so hot for him, then. I was, okay. God, he's such a *man*. But I don't . . ."

This was key.

". . . I don't want him asking me for any more details."

"*What?*"

"Well, he does!"

"About what?"

"My family. And where I'm from. You know. Faggot questions. He won't tell me what he does but he wants to know what I was like in sports when I was a kid. That's really neat!"

"All right, all right."

"Yeah, I really want to talk about it, don't I?"

"All right!"

"Yeah." He went over to the piano and picked out the right hand of the *Moonlight Sonata*. "'Some for me,'" he repeated, shaking his head. "You know why everyone's in San Francisco? Because this town is a madhouse. It is a *madhouse!*"

"So I hear. Eric says—"

"Just listen, okay?"

I shut up.

"He kisses me . . ." Carlo regarded me, considering. Maybe he shouldn't tell me. But he goes on: "He holds me down when he kisses me. On top of me. Listen." He left the piano, gazing at his hands, trying to show me what Daniel's hands do. "He kisses like he's eating you up—or no, *drinking* me, gulping me down. Like . . . I'm a glass of punch and he's going to drink me and then go out for seconds somewhere." He turned his hands over. "No. No . . . Only me. He only drinks me. That's what makes it so . . . I can't even breathe. When I pull away to gasp for air he grabs my head and holds me there and goes on drinking me up. He won't let me breathe!"

No, I was wrong before. *This* was key.

"When I first met him, you know what I thought he was? Don't laugh."

I waited.

"A knight. You know, in shining armor? A *hero*."

"Isn't he, now?"

Carlo showed me his hands again, how they hold him down. "If he's a hero, why won't he tell me what he does?"

"Maybe he wants you to guess."

"'Some for me!' Do you believe that?"

"Meanwhile, if you don't see him again, what will he do?"

"Oh, he's just bugging me. He's making a case."

"Are you afraid?"

"Of what?"

"So you aren't." But your days of carefree love are over, I thought, and you will know fear in time—because Chatty Cock is no match for Murder Cock.

I knew a little fear myself when Daniel called me to ask if we could meet. I feared scanting the etiquette by talking to him—it was Carlo, after all, to whom I owed fealty.

"I think not," I said.

"In the open," he urged. "Wherever you want. What could happen?"

I agreed, finally, to connect with him downtown in Footlight Records, a treasure house of old collectibles and an ideal meeting haunt because the later my associate, the more time I have to parse my sections of devotion. Records are my vice. But Daniel was standing outside when I got there. I

dragged him in, though he was obviously eager to talk, and—
while I don't enjoy Collecting with someone breathing over
my shoulder, whether of or against the sport—I tried to make
a game of it.

"Look!" I said, holding up an album. "The June Bronhill
Bitter Sweet!"

Daniel put a gloved hand on my shoulder and I turned
around. He looked at me; only that, but that sufficed. So I
took a deep breath and went outside with him to find some
lunch. Just don't charm me, I silently warned him. I'm doing
this for Carlo.

Well, you know these dangerous men can be very attrac-
tive across a table from someone they want something from.
Daniel wanted me to give a dinner so he could get hold of
Carlo again. "I just want to talk to him," he said.

"You'll have to tell him what you do."

"I intend to. I always meant to, right along. But he's delicate. He doesn't look it, but he is. The trouble with Carlo is,
he . . . he lacks inexperience. He never learned the hard way,
like most of us. He likes the same thing every time. The easy
thing. And he could be so . . . so *wild.*" Daniel spills this out
calmly as he sips coffee. Sure, let's all talk about our sex lives.
"He's a very hot man. But he stabilizes. Now, I say the interesting thing about taking a lover is letting him expand your
sensuality. *De*stabilize. Love isn't forever, anyway. Why not
make an adventure of it?"

So that was the missing piece after all: Carlo didn't want
to be on his back with someone who gets so much out of
being on top. It's innocuous, even amusing, with a switch-
hitting buddy. But with Murder Cock one may feel plun-
dered.

"The odd thing," he went on, "is when I first picked him
up, I took him for a man who would do anything. He looks
like a sort of degenerate saint."

"You're too smart for him."

"There's no such thing."

"You're like a lot of people I know. You verbalize."

"Don't you?"

"Sure. And I worry Carlo, too. You see, he thinks it's bad luck to know about something. He thinks it's good luck to do it."

"I can't live that way."

"Morals, politics, death, and feelings."

He sipped coffee and looked at me, considering what occult antecedent might have inspired that declaration. "I'm a policeman," he said.

"I don't catch the metaphor."

"Literally. That's what I do."

I was startled silent for a good twenty seconds. Then all I could say was "Good grief."

"See?" he said. "That's why I keep it a secret. I'm the best friend of all the men I have no use for, and the natural enemy of all the ones I like. Don't get me wrong: I'm on the right side. I just don't care for my teammates."

"That's politics and morals."

"You can joke about it because you don't live it. You're not on a team. You work alone."

Except for my neighbor, I thought.

"But, I'll tell you, everyone who sees me in uniform thinks I'm a hundred things I'm not and refuses to imagine the things I am. Think about it. What if you had to go around as a . . ." He searched.

"A commissar?"

He eyed me sagely. "We understand each other, don't we?"

"Not entirely. Policeman are a universal gay fantasy. Half the culture dreams of being arrested and treated to the protocols of interrogation. You have it made."

"That's just it, right there," he said heavily. "I'm not a fantasy. I'm a man, like you, like Carlo, like your fathers and brothers. I don't want to have to arrest my lovers."

"You're a person."

"Exactly."

"That's feelings. Three down, one to go."

98

"Look, I'm proud of what I do, and I'm tired of trying to talk my fellow gays into being proud for me. Look . . ."

"Look."

"Are you going to help me or not?"

"If you hadn't told me this, I wouldn't have done. I have to respect what Carlo wants. But I believe he'll want to see you again, on one condition—you have to come in uniform."

"Why?"

"Trust me."

He thought it over. "What could I do in uniform that I can't do out of it?"

"For one thing, you could have arrested the man with the knife instead of just neutralizing him."

He folded his hands on the table and looked at me.

"Is that my neck between your fingers?" I asked.

"I just want to tell you one thing. I'm very fond of Carlo. He's a very, very beautiful man. A beautiful man. If this doesn't work, I may want to neutralize you."

"I wonder if a New York City police officer should speak to a citizen of New York in that manner."

"Policemen are like everyone else. We break our oaths to make an effect."

"Anyway, that's all four, isn't it?"

So, on a night that timed to Daniel's schedule of patrols and breaks, I gave a dinner, the only one I give: Tree Tavern frozen pizza, spruced up with extra cheese, ketchup, oil, and oregano, and martyred in a raging oven for dark crust. I think the recipe (my mother's) is older than I am. With the most banal possible green salad, a boisterous dessert, and a lot of liquor, it'll do; anyway the people I know like pizza.

If Carlo was uncommunicative before the meal and tac-iturn during it, he was dead silent when Daniel walked in. In fact, he was stunned. Indeed, Daniel was a policeman. In his blues and accoutrements he looked . . . well, yes, stunning—like a knight. A hero. Dennis Savage exhaled audibly and Little Kiwi whispered, "Oh, yikes!" Diplomatically, I rattled on and then ran down, and there was absolute quiet. The rest of us watched Carlo, who looked like the little boy who would pray, "Oh God, make me good, but not yet."

"Are those handcuffs real?" Little Kiwi finally asked Daniel.

"They sure are. Want to try them?"

"I'm not allowed to. I'm glad you're back, though. You're not dangerous, are you, Daniel?"

"Only to bad guys."

Bauhaus doesn't fit under my couch, so on his unfortunately frequent visits he sits in the bathroom and barks if anyone tries to get in, or if anyone doesn't. Now he barked.

"Do you want me to tell you the alias of Inspector Wilberforce's canine wonder," Little Kiwi asked, "never yet revealed?"

"I wish you would."

Little Kiwi gave a stage whisper into Daniel's ear that could be heard clear to Baker Street. "They call him Secret Mantis."

Daniel looked at Little Kiwi for a bit, then took him by the arms and said, "Inspector, if you weren't securely accommodated with Dennis Savage here, I'd really worry about what would happen to you."

Little Kiwi looked up at him. "Why?"

"Because there are men who would spot you and cart you home and treat you real tough."

"And hit me?"

Carlo laughed. It was the first noise he had made since Daniel had joined us. He laughed so long that he held himself, and dropped his dessert plate, and made a mess, until Daniel was standing over him, and pulled him up, and Carlo held Daniel back, but he stayed near him and felt his badge and read out the number on it. Then he said, "Okay. But this time you can be Carlo. You."

Daniel nodded. "Midnight again."

Carlo said, "Yes. Again."

Daniel shook hands with all of us one by one—with Lit-

tle Kiwi he pretended to groan and hold his hand in pain—
and left.

"Is that why he had a gun, after all?" asked Little Kiwi.
"Just that?"

I nodded.

"And doesn't like the U.N.?"

I said, "Only Communazis and their dupes like the
U.N.," a remark that has enlivened many a party. This was
not a political group, however, and my words landed un-
challenged.

"But how can he be Carlo?"

"How can you be Inspector Wilberforce?"

Carlo's eyes clouded as he thought of something.

"Look at him," I told them. "He's had his first taste of an
Imaginary Lover."

"What?" said Carlo, but dimly.

"You've made a breakthrough," said Dennis Savage.
"Apparently."

"No," Carlo replied. "I always knew about this."

"About what?" asked Little Kiwi.

"About," I answered, "what Carlo is. And what his
lovers are. And why they ask faggot questions—though I've
always thought sex itself is the highest form of inquiry."

Carlo looked at me, and shook his head.

"And," I went on, "he is getting to know about fantasy."

"I don't believe in fantasy," said Carlo.

"'I must see the Things, I must see the Men,'" I exulted.

"Who said that?" asked Little Kiwi.

"Edmund Burke."

"Who's Edmund Burke?"

"Well, who are you, for that matter?"

Secret Mantis, the canine wonder, thrust his head out of
the bathroom, cagily watching.

"I'm Inspector Wilberforce, as is well known," Little
Kiwi explained. "But we don't know who you are."

"Yes," said Dennis Savage, coming up behind Little Kiwi

and putting his arms around him. Carlo, still half-dazed by the revelation of the uncertain in the familiar—and is this not what the Imaginary Lover is?—slowly joined them, putting his arms around Dennis Savage. "Now tell us, my friend," Dennis Savage pursued. "Who are you?"

"Well," I said, "sometimes I think I'm Edmund Burke."

And Eric Said
He'd Come

Christopher, an opera director with a twin brother who is also an opera director, invites me to a cottage by the sea. His friend Helen has taken a place in the Grove for a week; they want scintillating company. I'll do my best.

I met Helen once, at the Met. Inside of twenty seconds she asked what my middle name is, where I got that tie, how I met Christopher, if I knew where the Wagnerian contralto Ottilie Metzger died, and if she could try on my dark glasses.

I never turn down an invitation to Fire Island. Christopher met me at the ferry, where I feigned the necessary suave. I had dressed precisely, as if for a sacred pageant set on the sand, which, in fact, is what the Island of Fire is. In gray corduroy shorts, striped T-shirt, Mickey Mouse watch, running shoes, and punk socks, I'm so *right* that if there were grapefruit sections in my hair, I'd start a fad. Think hot to be hot.

Helen greets me warmly, on the deck of a trim little thing of a house on the ocean, west of the Monster. There is another guest, one Larry.

"Welcome to the D-list," he tells me. "You realize we're the only people in the Grove under sixty-five!"

Christopher laughs. Helen glowers. I'm bemused.

"The *Grove!*" he cries. As if to say: "The Black Hole of Calcutta!"

"What's for lunch?" I ask, to cue in the next scene.

"Decay. Ugliness. Stupidity." Larry marches off to the

beach, I presume to head for the Pines. Dire on a dune, he
adds, "If you can't get into hell, they send you here." Exit.

Silence.

"Good grief," I explain.

"I forgot to warn you about Larry," says Christopher.

"Whose friend *is* that?" I ask.

Helen and Christopher share accusing looks.

"Never mind," I tell them.

Helen can't let it rest. "The worst of it," she begins—
then checks herself, looks away, goes out the front door and
immediately surges in through the back—"The worst of it is:
he's *such a* schmarotzer!"

"Helen," Christopher begins.

"But your friend must be thirsty from his trip. Quick, a
tea, some cheese wedges, a boiled egg. Schmarotzer means
'parasite.' The Nazis used it against the Jews, as if they were
cultural parasites battening on Goethe, Schiller, Brentano,
without contributing anything of their own. *Battening!* I would
mention Heine and Mendelssohn. I lived in Germany for two
years. Munich."

"Why is Larry a schmarotzer?" I asked, feeling my way
into a new word.

Helen became tragic. She looked off to a remote pros-
pect—the colored frieze atop the facade of the Munich Staats-
oper, I imagined.

"He comes and he takes, and he takes, and he takes,"
Helen observes.

"He brought fruit," Christopher puts in. "He made pasta
primavera."

"With marinara sauce!"

Helen dramatically reveals a tub of cold rigatoni, stained
red amid broccoli and cauliflower. "The last supper of a
schmarotzer!" she screams.

"Egad," I say, to fill in a pause.

Now Helen is quiet, showing us what patience looks like.
"Does he offer anything to the group? Tell me that, please!"
She turns to me. "And he has the nerve—no, I can't! It's *too*

104

much!" She claps a hand to her mouth, but it flies right off again. "He had the nerve to ask for *Irish Coffee!*" She bustles to the fridge. "Now, there's five kinds of cheese . . ."

Eventually, I note that planning a cheese tray is Helen's most constant activity. Christopher has taken to calling her the Cheese Gräfin, and I join him. She seems to like it, or any kind of attention. It's hard to give her as much as she wants, though, as she never stops attending herself—asking, remarking, planning, promising. At length, in a daze, she says, "I must do the dishes," though the sink is empty.

Ottilie Metzger died at Auschwitz.

After lunch I excused myself for a solo flight in the Island manner and headed for the Pines, my favorite place. Here I learned to admire or tell off, here comprehended the pride of the beauty and the passion of the troll, here conceived the classes of gay and learned the nuances that separate tough from stalwart. I was a kid here, and grew wise. There are a number of stories that are assigned to each gay man's collection whether or not he'll have them: "The Day I Told My Parents," for instance, or "What I Saw in the Bars." There are perhaps fifteen such titles, and I think it notable that while those with an urban, rural, business, or family setting can take place anywhere in America with acceptable resonance, every beach story must take place on Fire Island. For here we find gay stripped to its essentials. The beautiful are more fully exposed here, the trolls more cast out than anywhere else—thus their pride and passion. The beguiling but often irrelevant data of talent and intelligence that can seem enticing in the city are internal contradictions in a place without an opera house or a library. Only money and charm count. Professional advantages are worthless, for, in a bathing suit, all men have the same vocation. Yet there are distinctions of rank. Those who rent are the proletariat, those who own houses are the bourgeoisie, and houseboys form the aristocracy.

Of course you cannot tackle the place alone.

Here you learn to focus your view of the scene. You decide which options you will take—say, toward fashion or naturalism, favoring colleagues or competition, dealing in aggressiveness or self-protection. It is too extreme to say that one's first trips to the Island will govern the rest of one's life in gay; but if it isn't true, it should be. New Yorkers virtually come out in this place. Every other gay beach is a strip of sand, merely theatre. But the Pines is a culture, really life.

There are three rules: You must let a veteran squire you about on the first jaunts, you must take to it gradually, and you must find your gang and join it. You *cannot* tackle the place alone.

Helen's "Does he offer anything to the group?" resounds in my head; suddenly I run smack into Eric, ensconced with friends between Pines and Grove. Between: as if respecting fashion but resenting it. Fearful of the sun, Eric is swaddled like an Arab. All I can see are his eyes, nose, and mouth. He is thrilled that I materialize by chance, for anything that wants to occur by arrangement unnerves him. "And Eric said he'd come" is this famous, useless remark we make at parties, our voices trailing off as we survey a dismal gathering that needs an Eric.

Once, a wicked friend envisioned satirical Ph.D theses for all the famous gay writers. A lapidarian storyteller and essayist got "The Use of Style in Filling a Vacuum." A veteran of pre-Stonewall got "Beauty and Truth: The Positioning of Jeans in My Dust Jacket Photos." Unfair, I thought, but I laughed. Eric, by miles the best writer of the lot, got "The Swank and the Drab: Philosophy and Technique." Yet here he was, hiding from both the swank and the drab, hiding *between,* as if instituting a new sort of gay in which neither praise nor blame will be freely given. A quiet place, this, just around the corner from the turmoil of keeping up with Jones, with his Chelsea lats, Perry Ellis sleeves, and Greek tan.

I tell Eric of the schmarotzer and the Cheese Gräfin. He is mildly fascinated, but mainly he wants an ice-cream cone. I feel I should get back to my house. We decide to drop Eric's things off at his friends', head for downtown Grove for ice cream, and then . . . but he won't plan farther ahead. He may stay over in the Grove. He may return to the Pines, where he spent last night with a group of queens so ritualized that their place is known as "the house of good taste and bad manners." Then, again, he may simply vanish. He is always in flight, fearful of fame, and seldom seen.

On the way to ice cream we pass the baroque guest house called Belvedere, where a gorgeous blond houseboy stares balefully about him.

"A beauty in the Grove," we murmur. "How bitter he seems." Who wouldn't be, here? "What does he bring to the group?" I almost ask, thinking of Larry the schmarotzer. Larry had spoken of "Pines People" and "Grove People"; but only the losers divide the world into winners and losers. You cannot redeem yourself by joining the people who—you think—hate you.

Eric suffers a raptus of indecision when we hit the ice-cream stand—should he buy a sandwich in the grocery instead? He does, and there we meet the Gräfin, her basket filled with goodies. She's thrilled to meet Eric and insists he join us for drinks. "Blueberries," she cries, showing us. "I thought we'd have them with sweet cream." And "Cheeses!" she reveals. "Do you want biscuits or crackers with them?" Ensues a pause as Eric and I try to remember what the difference is. "I'll get both!" she vows.

I gather that Christopher also stole away; the Gräfin hopes to lure us back with tasties. Surprisingly, Eric wants to come. "It's the blueberries," he tells me. "Only food impels me now." He is worried, though, about meeting the schmarotzer. He doesn't want to confront the injured nagging of the disinherited gay, that terror born of taking one's reading at others' evaluations. It reminds me of a few unpublished writers I have met, who believe there is a conspiracy to keep them out of the top houses, the hot magazines.

Actually, no one thinks about them whatsoever.

"The schmarotzer is Pines bound," I tell Eric, "and now he is out of the saga." Eric smiles and looks away. He imagines that half the things I say are allusions to obscure lit that only I would be mad enough to read. He is intent on the blueberries, and refuses to speak of anything else. "How many will she let me have?" he wonders.

"She's so impressed with who you are that she'd give you the box."

References to his public radiance disenchant him; now he won't talk at all. But he's *thinking* of blueberries.

Christopher has returned, and we drink tequila with lemon while waiting for the Gräfin to accommodate us. Christopher works hard when he directs opera, but at socializing he turns himself way down, seldom talking and scarcely listening. We have been friends since college, some fourteen years now, and have long since accepted each other without qualification.

It is not a dangerous relationship, and I wonder if that is enviable or pitiable.

The Gräfin returns with her groceries and we cheer. Eric gets ready. But for once she does not produce a tray. She unpacks in the kitchen, as noisily as possible—do I actually hear her calling out the items as she unloads?—but joins us with nothing in hand.

Eric is worried.

The Gräfin asks if Eric will stay for dinner, asks again, urges—he is evasive throughout—and I suddenly realize that she is using the blueberries as incentive. Hopeless. Promising to come by tomorrow if he's still here, Eric beats his retreat. The Gräfin is startled. It is her habit, whenever someone is leaving, to call out hysterical attempts to detain him—dire requests, pathetic mandates, whimpers of pain, anything. It is a relatively minor maneuver in the practice of high kvetching. Eric will have none of it. He smiles, says something wonderful, and goes.

"Will he come to dinner?" Helen asks me.

"I think not."

"He offers," she sighs, "so much to the group."

"You promised him blueberries."

"For dessert!"

"You made it sound as if the blueberries were hors d'oeuvres."

"Blueberries for hors d'oeuvres!" Christopher cries in mock society-horror. "What would Lady Gumbo say?"

I went walking through the Grove to think. Every time I stay in the Pines I have epiphanies and adventures; in the Grove I just have a stay at the beach. It's like the Jersey shore gone gay. There's no group there to offer anything to.

But the Pines one must join. Is this why it has its outraged detractors? Were they not invited to belong? A friend of mine denigrated the Pines in favor of the Grove, till one day a friend of his bought a ritzy house in the Pines with a pool on the ocean: and very quickly and quietly the Pines-hater transferred his affections.

The Pines gives back what you offer, no more. You don't come out looking like Fatso McDump, knowing no one anyone wants to know, and expect to be crowned King of the Pines. Yes, there is more beauty gathered here than elsewhere, and the beach insistently reveals it; so is this elation or despair? Does the congregation of dream palazzi with their two-story love dens under skylights of stars reproach you for lack of swank?

I think the Pines is friendly. It is young, and was founded on elation; the Grove died years ago, in despair. It is never inclusive or convivial, as the Pines routinely is; of course a beauty is bitter in Belvedere—in the Grove, beauty is suspect. How often I would trade hellos with some dazzling stranger as we passed on the Pines boardwalk. Never once did this happen in the Grove.

Till now. I was wearing a Yale T-shirt, light blue with the letters in huge white blocks across my chest, and one of those swank workmen who are forever tooling along the planks in motor carts suddenly stopped and called out, "Is that Yale for real?"

"Surest thing you know," I answered.

"Harvard, '61," he said, smiling. He looked too young to be class of '61—maybe he meant he was born at Harvard in '61. "It's a small world."

"That it is." I smiled back, and off he went.

Well, it's a loose confederation to make a coincidence of, but 'twill serve. I felt chipper when I got back, and, as Christopher was out, I took the Gräfin to tea in the Pines, proudly leading her through the Grove like L'Enfant touring friends about D.C. At Belvedere, she stopped and stared at the place, at the empty courtyard, the dizzy pile, the discreet nameplate. Eric and I had rushed past, panicked by the angry houseboy who knew he was in the wrong place. The Gräfin pauses to take this wonder in. "Belvedere," she reads out, looking through the gratings at the turrets and gingerbread. "Belvedere," she repeats, listening to the sound. "Not Jewish." She shrugs and moves on.

"Why do you make such a big deal about religion, Helen?" I ask. "Are you forming a club?"

"The club is already formed."

We were passing into the Judy Garland Memorial Park that lies between Grove and Pines. I'm never sure exactly where I'm going through all those paths and copses—Eric can do it in the dark—but we glided along without a step wasted, arriving at tea just after seven.

"Will you know many people?" The Gräfin asks as we snake around the cut of the harbor. She senses that Eric is a celeb, and it takes one to know one. "I may know some," I say doubtfully.

I know one, in the event: Michael, one of my publishers, who has the sexiest hair in lit. Michael knows everyone. The Gräfin is thrilled to meet him, too, but Michael is taken aback when the Gräfin tells him she never reads; reading is highest calling to Michael. As the talk proceeds, the Gräfin wanders off, and moments later I see her engaged in conversation with a stranger. You have to admit, she has nerve. Rejoining us, she says, "That is Bob the Accountant. Very nice. But I suddenly remembered that I have to take my mother's jewelry out of the bank and wear it every so often." She turns to Michael. "Do you prefer the necklace? Or the ring?"

Michael looks at us as if we were a mountebank and his zany, stirring up a medieval plaza for strolling theatricals. Still, he invites us to drinks at his house on Beachcomber, on the way back to the Grove. The Gräfin celebrates by picking up Bob the Accountant once again on our way along the boardwalk.

Michael looks back at them, as if to say, "What *is* this?" He's too polite to ask, but I answer anyway: "Helen is very into non sequitur, but she has a sweet heart." It sounds like the first line of the last hundred novels Michael rejected.

Michael has a palazzo. The entree takes one up to the kitchen, where we meet one of the most Nordic-looking people I've ever seen, shirtless, tending a huge pan of chicken breasts. Michael introduces him as Erhart. Helen disengages Bob the Accountant at the very doorstep, which I think is strangely cute. But after one look at Erhart, she parks herself outside the kitchen window and stares.

I think of her words outside Belvedere: "Not Jewish." Erhart stirs the chicken, noting Helen, as Michael pulls out glasses and vodka. Finally she speaks, and what she asks Erhart is:

"Is that your bar mitzvah watch?"

"Helen," I warn her, "no kvetching." I turn to Erhart. *"Wollen Sie Deutsch sprechen mit dieser Frau, Erhart? Sie hätte es gern."*

Erhart looks confused. "I am Swiss," he says. It sounds relevant, but it isn't.

The Gräfin has entered the house. "Is that tarragon chicken?" she asks. "You speak English very well for a Swiss."

"I am not Swiss," he says. Erhart, *please!* (It later turns out that he means that his parents are Swiss, but he is total American, and speaks no German.)

Michael shows us the house. Quel palazzo—and guess who owns it? Erhart. It has a pool, a superb viewing aerie on the roof, separate decks for each bedroom, and a sunken conversation nook.

How would Larry the schmarotzer feel if he were here? Better? Famous? Included?

The nook is so comfortable that I decide that the combined cow-hurling teams of Zürich, Bern, and Luzern won't move me, but the Gräfin, as always, is restless. Away we go, then, racing down the beach through that virulent wind that patrols the space between Pines and Grove. "He's so warm!" the Gräfin screams of Michael as we run the sand. "He makes you feel as if you'd known him all your life!"

No, Helen, I carefully fail to say. He is, like anyone with will and intelligence, heedless of those without it. Everything is forgivable but non sequiturs; the strong warm to the other strong. We stagger through the Grove, drunk on swank, and find Christopher inside on the couch, reading in the dark— indeed, holding his book up to the window to catch light that went dead an hour before.

He has eaten all the blueberries.

Still, we have a merry time, high on tequila sunrises, planning a cookout, and making up risible songs. The Gräfin sings "Surabaja Larry" and "Un bel dì, Schmarotzer," and Christopher and I use *Schmarotzendiva* and *Schmarotzenkunst* in every sentence. It's a little like a Boy Scout Jamboree, eating hamburgers under the stars and singing around the dying embers of the campfire. Except at a Jamboree you're not allowed to be silly. I wonder if I should be having quite so good a time on a sexless jaunt to a sexual paradise; when I'm forty, I bet, I'll regret having missed every single opportunity to score.

The Gräfin, at least, is having a ball, raving over the view from Michael's roof and instructing me to get into that house next summer so as to invite everyone out. Even Erhart, by the chemistry of the Gräfin's self-delusion, has become an icon, a collectible. The Gräfin is telling Christopher he could not hope to eat such chicken as Erhart cooked; but she never tasted it.

112

ema, most likely French: two writers perched on a kind of bleachers, watching and commenting as birds of rare plumage stalk past.

"Do you by any chance remember . . ." I begin, then stop; he is already shaking his head and smiling. He never remembers what I remember. We entertain contrary nostalgias, even for Pines weekends we spent in each other's company. I was going to ask him if he recalled an afternoon when we sat way far back against the dune pickets. The beach was empty and the wind tart. Even in sweatshirts we were shuddering. I had just told Eric that *A la Recherche du Temps Perdu* was the only great book I had never read and he was testing this with other possibilities. He jumped from Frank Norris to Petronius to Flaubert; still, he couldn't trip me up. Then he was silent, determined to find a sure thing. At last he spoke, with the ring of triumph: "*The Man Without Qualities!*"

"Do you really think that's a great book?"

Just then a man we knew of from the Eagle's great old days walked into our line of vision. He, too, had been there on my first night, and like the rest of us was there on most other nights too, a golden-blond hero who, for some of us, was kind of a poster for gay: Join up and you'll look like this. Now his hair was almost gone and his famous stomach had given way to creeping metabolic slowdown, yet he moved as if he still had it. Somewhere off to the right, we heard a woman's voice calling, "Kokomo! Kokomo!" A cocker spaniel came running up to the man, who knelt to pet him as he frolicked. "Kokomo!" the woman insisted. The dog at last obeyed and ran off. The man saw us as he rose, recognized us from the old days, and, though we had never spoken to him in our lives, shot us a marvelous smile and waved as he turned to go.

"Harvard, '61," I murmur, thinking of this.

"What?" says Eric.

"Nothing."

I wonder how long it will be before the threatened beach erodes right up to the house line.

I consider what I offer to the group.

I eat my sandwich.

"'Do you *have* to be here?'" I echo. "That's a good question, isn't it?"

"What happened to the blueberries?" Eric asks.

At the ferry slip he gets into a confusion over the possibility of an ice-cream cone. I buy one; he doesn't.

And the ferry glides into the harbor, filled—as my little brother Tony used to say—to the grim. Except no: everyone's smiling, expectant, tolerant. It's exciting to be here. As the boat passes the tea crowd, a few people wave, some wave back, someone calls out a real name like Jim or Steve, more people wave and others cheer, the ferry toots a whistle, and now everybody is cheering from the island to the boat and back. Everyone is waving and smiling.

"Do we have to be here?" I asked Eric as we climbed to the ferry's upper deck. "We ought to, yes. But do we have to?"

"Isn't that the Cheese Gräfin?" he asked, pointing.

It was: sitting at the dock, watching, forlorn.

"Where's Christopher?" I asked.

Eric waved.

The Gräfin watched.

Now I waved. "Helen!" I called. "Helen!"

She watched.

"Why is she there?" Eric asked.

"To see us off in a kvetching manner."

At last she waved, a sad, fulfilled wave of the most thorough good-bye. There would be, she seemed to acknowledge, no Michael house next summer, no more Jamboree. *Her* story ends here. But there was Christopher, lapping a cone. You cannot tackle the place alone.

The tea crowd cheered us as we floated by.

"Whom are you waving at?" Eric mused.

"At the gay community."

We looked back at the dock. Helen and Christopher had vanished.

"The swank and the drab," I told Eric, "and all between."

"There is nothing," he said in mock queen, "between swank and drab except early-middle Nazi punk."

"You sound like one of your characters."

"Was that an insult or a compliment?"

"Everything I've ever said to you or about you, in your whole life, is a compliment."

"Yah." He nods vigorously, looks away, hates hearing that, more praise to suffer.

And what I'm thinking is, If I use him in a story, he'll probably never speak to me again.

The Shredding of
Peter Hawkins

My fourth best friend fell in love for the first time in his life when he was thirty-four.

"Ridiculous," someone told me. "Peter's too shallow to love."

"Disaster," said another. "No one that layered should do an affair."

"Heaven," a third pronounced it. "When you ask him what he's been doing he smirks like the Mona Lisa. And *have you seen the boyfriend?*"

"He'll be lacerated!" Dennis Savage exulted. "That ersatz Clark Gable in Speedos! He'll writhe and shriek like a rat in a Skinner box! He'll be shredded, and I hope I'm there to see it!"

"Has love shredded you and Little Kiwi?"

"No, because we're flexible. You have to give in all the time. You have to be humiliated and abused and it hurts like wild. Peter Hawkins thinks he can do it scot-free. Love without tears! That's like dessert without fat! Oh, just wait." He was whispering now, almost cackling, like the Wicked Witch dunking the poisoned apple. Tasty. Delicious. "Just wait."

I wouldn't have long to wait, because Dennis Savage, Little Kiwi, and I were about to share a house in the Pines with Peter and a fifth individual (contracted on the phone by Little Kiwi) who for unknown reasons never turned up when we were there. We put it down to sound social planning, and asked no more about it, though our mystery housemate left a trace here and there, especially in the pantry. It was a handsome house, by Pines standards. Significant others included Little Kiwi's possibly extraterrestrial dog, Bauhaus, and Peter's boyfriend, The Incredible Jeff McDonald.

Jeff was then living out the last years of his legend; one more little epoch and he would fade into the background of an Edward Hopper. But even at forty-some-odd he retained everything that had made him notable: a handsomeness that inspired cries of "Eureka!" from Morton Street Pier to the Thalia; a lazy walk that not five in a thousand could imitate; and thighs of, literally, death: once you glimpsed them, if you could not have them for your own, you died. In the 1970s, during High Middle Eagle and Tenth Floor Culture, everyone knew his name, but few knew him, for he wasn't a flirt. He was a lover.

I thought he'd be good for Peter, experienced and patient and maybe a bit worn down. Beginners don't usually handle an affair well, but veteran Jeff could ease Peter over the Three Fatal Mistakes in Romance: being late, being bored, and being hurt. I wondered, though, who would help Jeff deal with Peter's First Principle of Rational Living: being private.

"Always hold something back," he would tell me, "or they'll keep taking and taking."

"Who's they?" I asked.

"Little secrets build up your personal space. And make your associates make sense. We must admire the clarity of reason."

Peter lived for reason and personal space. Once his phone rang while I was visiting, and, consulting his watch, he told me, "This will be my mother, asking if I got the invitation to Cousin Patty's wedding and am I going."

It was. He got it. And no, he wasn't going—*because she asked.* "I've told you over and over, if you harass me about family things I won't attend them. . . . It's no use whining. . . . Nor will I give in to emotional blackmail. Yes, you are pushing. It's irritating, boring, and stupid. So give up because you can't win."

119

He shook his head as he rang off. "Some people simply cannot admire the clarity of reason."

Speaking as one who also suffers from wedding-crazed parents, I could admire the clarity of Peter's reason. But I wondered how it felt to be his mother.

I wondered, too, how Jeff would take to Peter's mode of living. One forgives much at the start of an affair; we are tough only with perfect strangers and imperfect intimates. So Jeff tolerated going to dinner alone because Peter had to catch up on some "unsharable" friend, or getting no answer when he phoned at midnight, or learning that Peter would not join him at a Mets game, period. "Baseball is for jerks," is how Peter put it; and Jeff took it.

I agree, I confess. Football and tennis are for sports, and baseball calls for a nerd's sensibility. Still, I had to ask Peter if he hadn't been a little hard on Jeff.

"In fact, no," Peter replied. "I don't drag him along to the theatre, do I?"

"Maybe he'd enjoy being dragged."

"He'd be bored, and he wouldn't like me as much anymore because I'd be boring him. He's a wonderful man, and I truly love him. Truly. You see, I'm not afraid to say so. It's . . . it's a miraculous thing, love. But it must be understood, and kept within reasonable bounds. It does not make sense for me to suffer through baseball games or for Jeff to suddenly have to like Stephen Sondheim. He just isn't cultured, and I am, and we have to work around that."

"What if . . . ?" I didn't have the heart to go on. Poor blind boy, I thought; are you in for trouble.

"What if what?" He was smiling, content that he had learned love's call number and could phone up as it suited him.

"What if love doesn't see reason? What if Jeff says, 'Come to a Mets game or else'?"

Peter mulled that over for a bit. "That won't happen," he said finally, yet with perhaps somewhat less than his usual authority. "He likes me too much to do that."

120

I nodded as uncommittedly as possible, the way you'd be polite on Mars.

"Well, doesn't he?" Peter asked.

"I know that you two are very much involved with each other. And I wish you a flawless romance."

He decided to accept that as agreement, and The Summer of Peter and Jeff began.

I would date the absolute first moment of this particular story to a Pines afternoon in mid-June. Jeff and I were on the deck tasting my favorite childhood treat, potato-chip sandwiches, when Peter ambled up looking breezy. Jeff asked, "Where have you been?" and Peter replied, "Nowhere," and Jeff said, "Where is nowhere?" and Peter said, "What difference does it make?" and Jeff countered with "It makes a difference to me," and Peter asked, "Why?" and I wished that a giant eagle would swoop down and carry me away. Or no, a winged Italian mesomorph with vulnerable eyes; but I'd take an eagle.

"I don't want you walking off on me," said Jeff.

Peter sat down and began to eat the filling out of my sandwich. "What am I, your houseboy?"

"Where were you?"

"If you mean, was I cheating on you, you know I wasn't."

"You're damn straight I know you weren't."

"That's all you have to know."

"I'm late for my bolero lesson," I began.

"Don't go," said Peter. "This is not the first time this has happened. But it'll be the last." He turned to Jeff. "I went away. Now I'm back. It doesn't matter where I was. End of scene."

Howling and barking on the walk warned of the return of Dennis Savage and company. Jeff pulled his chair closer to Peter's. "If it doesn't matter, why keep it a secret?"

"If it doesn't matter, why do you have to know?"

"Where were you? And I mean it."

Peter folded his arms across his chest and sighed.

Little Kiwi ran up. "Bauhaus caught someone's Frisbee just like that dog in the commercial and raced off with it! Now they don't know where it is! I expect he buried it, but he won't tell." He examined Peter: sullen. He saw Jeff: mad. "Oh no," Little Kiwi whispered. "The first quarrel."

Dennis Savage plopped the grocery bags on the table with a groan. "How does beef stew grab you? With new potatoes."

No one spoke. Jeff gently rubbed Peter's neck, but Peter wouldn't look at him. Little Kiwi took the bags inside. Bauhaus fell off the deck into the poison ivy for about the twentieth time that weekend.

"That dog is such an asshole," said Dennis Savage. Then he noticed. "What's wrong?"

"Nothing's wrong," said Peter, trying to smile.

"One more time," said Jeff, slipping his arm around Peter's shoulder. "Where were you?"

"Please don't do this," Peter replied. "I'm loyal, clever, and cute. I'll never let you down. Never, I promise. Isn't that enough?"

"Nothing is enough," Jeff told him. "That's what love is. The more you have the more you need. You aren't halfway there yet."

Peter got up and started for the walk, calling out, "I'll be back for dinner." Brisk. Nonchalant. The Peter I know. At the turning he paused, came back, and looked Jeff in the eye. "Okay," he said. He took a deep breath. "Okay. I went to visit Tod Graham. His father has cancer. He needs visits. The house was full of people. Is that what you want? Is that enough now? Is that love?"

Bauhaus barked.

"Little Kiwi," Dennis Savage called out, "come get your idiotic dog out of the grunge."

"Yes, that's what I want," said Jeff.

Little Kiwi joined us, eyeing Peter and Jeff nervously. "Bauhaus, come!"

Bauhaus made a pass at the deck, missed, and whimpered.

Jeff went over to Peter. "It's silly to fight over something so small. Let's save the fights for the big issues."

"I don't want to fight at all."

"But we will."

"It hurts me when you fight." Peter was pleading: a strange Peter. "It *hurts* me, Jeff."

"It hurts me when you aren't honest."

Little Kiwi dragged the dog onto the deck. "Now he's full of cooties. I *told* you not to fall off, didn't I?"

"I *am* honest," said Peter. Tears were rolling down his cheeks.

Jeff took him in his arms.

I looked at Dennis Savage. He was somewhat less than thrilled to witness the shredding of Peter Hawkins, after all. "Little Kiwi, he said, "come help me zip up the salad."

Little Kiwi was watching Peter and Jeff like Emily Dickinson viewing the dismembering of a butterfly.

"Shoo," I told him.

He ran into the house.

For the next few days, Jeff and Peter played together like puppies. "It's always like that," Dennis Savage informed me, "after the first fight. But then comes the second, and the third. . . ."

"What a horror show," I cried. "We've seen Peter crying—Peter who mutes ghetto blasters with a look."

"Yes, that really scared you. Because if our strong, sensible Peter can cry, anyone can, right?"

"Who's anyone, as if I didn't know, you dreary plop who rims scrofulous sheep?"

"The day you fall in love, I will personally phone in the item to Liz Smith: BOY WRITER STRICKEN WITH CASE OF FEELINGS. CONDITION CRITICAL. WEEPING, MOPING, AND PICKING LISTLESSLY AT HIS ZWEIBACK AND MILK."

"I always knew you secretly hated me."

"First Peter, then you, and that'll be the end of you arrogant sons-of-bitches who think you can take it or leave it. You're going to die, boyo, just like the rest of us. I'm going to fix you up with death himself."

A pause ensued.

"You know," I said, "sometimes these jokes get a little out of control."

Yes. And he nodded. Yes.

Peter and Jeff did start quarreling again; by August it had become a routine of the house, something always going on, like MTV or construction noises. There was a lot of Why? and When? from Jeff, and rebuffs from Peter. Why won't you come to Dick's party? When did you get home last night? Why do we have to go to Europe for Thanksgiving? When a wall of silence failed to prove deterrent, Peter worked out a way to answer Jeff's queries without saying anything, and their bickering took on an absurdist note, like a play with every third line missing. "Why aren't you?" provoked responses like "But I am—or I shall have had to be, before long," or simply "Because I believe that you are Attila the Nun."

Jeff was exasperated and bewildered, unable to battle through these rebuses. But Peter reclaimed some of his old dash. He would not surrender to the fascism of romance again.

"I know what," said Little Kiwi one lunchtime. "Every day each of you has to tell one true thing that you never told anyone before."

"Is that how you and Dennis Savage survive?" asked Jeff.

"We don't have to," said Dennis Savage. "We're—"

"Flexible, we know," I put in, thinking that he's about as flexible as the Pope's hernia truss.

"Now, for example," Little Kiwi went on, "Jeff could say who Peter most reminds him of. And Peter could tell about the cutest thing Jeff ever did. Or something."

"The cutest thing Jeff ever did," said Peter, "was when

124

he forgot to clean out the medicine cabinet when his parents were visiting, and his mother came out of the bathroom and said—"

"Shut up!"

Peter, lean and mean, smiled. "You want me to be honest, don't you?" he said.

"And loyal, how about that?"

"Oh, no." Peter shook his head, snapped his fingers, pointed at Jeff. He had found the stop in reason's mind that would put love in its place. "Loyalty needs lying. Do you want me to be honest or loyal? It's one or the other."

"And what does Peter remind you of?" Little Kiwi asked Jeff, merrily, but with an edge.

Jeff grinned at Peter. "He reminds me of—"

"You remind me of the Elephant Man!"

"*You fucking zit!*"

"But we have to be nice to you because you've got a terminal case of brainturd, that dread disease in which your brain slowly turns into a great, big, brown—"

Jeff leaped out of his chair and went for Peter, who dodged around the table. "What other wonderful games can you suggest for us to play?" I asked Little Kiwi, as Peter and Jeff lunged about us.

"I know Animal Lotto," he answered.

Eventually Jeff heaved into his chair and told Peter to fuck off. Peter did so with a purposeful look in his eye, leaving a sober quartet to assess and attempt to make remedy.

"You have to stop fighting," Dennis Savage told Jeff. "You're the top-okay couple of the summer. They were fainting when you and Peter walked into tea yesterday. Fashion and ad people in the six figures are lining up for dinner invitations."

Jeff shrugged.

"Why did he call you the Elephant Man?" Little Kiwi asked.

"Why do you think?"

"Because you like peanuts?"

"Size."

Little Kiwi paused. "Size what?"

"Of his, uh, trunk," I said.

"Mere trivia," said Dennis Savage. "The issues are sharing and candor and that's exactly—Little Kiwi, stop gaping—where Peter can't compromise."

"Why does he have to?" I asked.

"Because I said so," said Jeff. You should have seen his face.

"I admit that Peter is a pretty unbending character," I went on, "but isn't that in itself good reason to run this affair by his rules? Keep company, but respect your differences. Share what is sharable."

"He's too mixed up even for that," said Jeff. "He's been covering his insecurity so long that he can't open up at all."

"Two men can't give up the same thing at the same time," I said.

Well, that stopped them.

"What happens in straight romance?" I continued. "The woman gives up her independence and the man gives up nothing. That's why they're man and wife, not husband and wife. She has to change, not he. She pays the compromises. But when two men couple, no one is giving up anything. That's bound to create tension, and some men can compensate for it better than others. Peter compensates less well."

"Bullshit."

"That's the retort of an ignorant lout. I expect something more sensitive from someone in love."

"Look!" Little Kiwi shouted, pointing at Ocean Walk. "An ox!"

"A deer. Specialty of the Pines."

Bauhaus strained at his rope, fuming and groaning.

"Hush, Bauhaus."

So Bauhaus promptly barks and the deer runs off.

"It's done all the time," Jeff repeats. "*I* do it. Why can't he?"

"Why don't you give him a chance to edge into it?" I asked.

"If it doesn't start right, it's already finished," Jeff retorted, flaring up. "He'll do what he has to, or I'll find out why but good!"

"You made him cry," Little Kiwi blurted out. "You're the Elephant Man!"

"Walk time," said Dennis Savage.

Little Kiwi eyed the boardwalk. "Do ox bite?"

"*Oxen* bite. Deer don't. Come." Away they went, Bauhaus dragging on his leash.

"That kid is very pretty," said Jeff, looking after them. "But real stupid."

"He's bright enough to know how to behave in love."

"And how is that?"

"With ease."

He took a deep breath, tilted his chair back, and watched me. "Let me tell you something," he finally said. "I've gone to and fro in love, and walked up and down in it. I know love. Peter doesn't. Nor do you. So he's going to take my advice, and you're going to keep yours to yourself."

"Think I'll catch up with the guys," I said, rising. "One thing, though: next time you use the Bible for your text, don't quote the devil. It hurts your credibility."

"What Bible?"

"'Going to and fro in the earth and walking up and down in it.' The Book of Job."

He chuckled. "I knew that was from somewhere."

Peter stayed away all that day and night and didn't return till just before dinner the next day. Little Kiwi insisted on making the drinks, which he called Kazootie Koolers: white wine drowning grapes, melon balls, and strawberries.

"I hope no one drops in and sees us drinking these," said Dennis Savage. "I mean, I like them, but they'd be hard to alibi to anyone on the A-list."

"Why don't you do what you want to do without reference to what others think?" I asked.

"Because no man is an island!"

"*I* am an island!"

"So am I," said Peter, strolling in. "I'm Fire Island." Nice. Assured. "I'm the embodied truth of the Pines. I'm the destiny of homoerotic passion." He marched into the house and came out munching a hunk of cheese. "Aren't you going to ask where I was?" he asked Jeff. "If it doesn't matter, why keep it a secret, right? So where was I?"

Jeff ignored him.

"Hey," Peter went on, "what would happen if I took Bauhaus for a run?"

"You best not," said Little Kiwi. "He's afraid of an ox."

Jeff got up.

"Do you want a Kazootie Kooler?" Little Kiwi asked Peter, his eyes on Jeff.

"Hell, yes."

Jeff confronted Peter.

"I was with Jim Guest," said Peter, quite casually. "All night. He's hotter than you are. Now you know and how do you like it?"

Jeff fetched Peter a walloping blow to the side of the head and knocked him flat on the deck.

To Bauhaus' crazed barking, Dennis Savage and I jumped between them. Jeff threw us one by one off the deck into the grunge. Bauhaus came, too; it's possible that he prefers it there.

Jeff pulled Peter to his feet and smacked him down again.

"I knew you'd be understanding about this," said Peter.

"How do I like it?" shouted Jeff. "How do I like it, huh?"

Now Little Kiwi got between them. "Go away!" he cried, harrying Jeff with his chair as one tames a tiger. "Go away *now!*"

"This is how I like it," said Jeff, pushing past Little Kiwi to get to Peter again. Dennis Savage and I had just gained the deck when we saw Jeff haul Peter up by the collar of his shirt and Little Kiwi punching Jeff in the back. Suddenly, someone said, "What the fruit is going on here?" and we turned to find the most nondescript man I've ever seen, standing on our deck holding an overnight bag and a briefcase. He was a pair of glasses with no eyes behind them.

"Which of you," he went on, "is Virgil Brown?"

"I am," said Little Kiwi.

"I'm Orville McKlung. Permit me to point out that you said nothing about violence when I inquired about the tenor of the house. Nor did you speak of a dog."

Bauhaus grumbled in the grunge.

The man walked past us into the house in the flat-footed but hip-rolling gait of the queen who believes that everyone thinks he's straight. We could hear him rummaging in the kitchen. Sniffing. Put out.

Outside, our riot collapsed. Little Kiwi picked up the fallen chair. Dennis Savage examined Peter's ear, which was bleeding. Jeff stood off a bit, not taking his eyes off Peter, not even to blink. A moment later, the stranger was back, flourishing a cookie wrapper.

"And who, may I ask, ate almost all my Lorna Doones?"

"I didn't know they were yours," said Peter.

"I saved them for tonight! It's my Wednesday night special!"

("That sounds like you," Dennis Savage murmured to me." "Your mother wears a dribble bib," I replied.)

"Would you like a Kazootie Kooler?"

"No, Mr. Brown, I would like my Lorna Doones replaced."

"*Mea culpa,*" said Peter. "I'll go."

"Let me," I said. His shirt was torn almost in two.

"Peter and I will go," said Jeff. "Together."

"I'm not going anywhere with you."

"Do you want more of the same?"

Peter held his ground. "I won't cry for you this time."

We all stood and waited, except Orville McKlung, who muttered, "Swindlers," and went inside.

"Come on," said Jeff, extending his hand.

"No!"

"If you don't take my hand," said Jeff, "I'm going to drag you to the store by the neck for all the Pines to see. And when the dish queens get through with you, you'll be the laugh of the week."

"I don't believe you," said Peter.

"Bud," said Jeff, his eyes still on Peter, "do you believe me?"

"I believe you would try," I answered.

"I hurt you," Jeff told Peter. "I'll hurt you again. And I'll be sorry then as I'm sorry now. But you hurt me, too. You've been hurting me since we met. That's what love is." Jeff seemed to circle around Peter, surround him. "Now, come with me and we'll buy this man his cookies, and then we'll take a walk on the beach and talk about it. I can make it up to you."

Peter laughed softly. "How could you possibly?"

"Tonight."

Peter paused, looked away, shook his head, let Jeff take his hand. "I don't love you anymore," he said dully.

"That's when you love me the most," Jeff told him. "When you feel it hurting."

"Somebody . . . please help me," said Peter.

Little Kiwi whispered, "I'll help you. What do you want?"

Peter looked at Jeff. "I want to go with him."

"You don't need any help for that," said Jeff.

And away the two of them went.

"You know what's funny about extroverts?" I said. "They're just as dogmatic as introverts."

"Did you hear the other guy call me 'Mr. Brown'?" said Little Kiwi.

"Speaking of that," said Dennis Savage, "whose idea was

130

it to let Little Kiwi arrange for the disposition of the shares in this house?"

"'Mr. Brown,'" Little Kiwi quoted, striking a solemn pose, "'I would like my Lorna Doones replaced.'"

"Little Kiwi, get that menace of a dog back among the living!"

Little Kiwi helped Bauhaus onto the deck and said, "Now everyone has cooties but me."

"That won't last long," replied Dennis Savage, as I pretended to fan myself like a deb at a more than usually intense prom.

And when anyone complains to me that he's getting old and has no romance, I think of Jeff and Peter, and remark that I know someone who didn't fall in love till he was thirty-four.

Think of all you have to look forward to.

A Christmas Carol

My family has been celebrating a highly traditional Christmas since before I was born. We trimmed no trees—Mother disdained them as fire hazards. But we did everything else Americans do, from rummaging through closets to see what presents were heading our way to gloating over them on Christmas Eve as my father took home movies and mother served champagne to those of age and caviar to all. I mean the real thing, too, on a multi-leveled tray bearing chopped, boiled egg, minced onion, sour cream, and toast. (When he thought no one was looking, my dad would slip a spoon into the fish and glop it down neat.) The caviar tray was as much a part of our Night Before as was staying up late with my brothers to reminisce, bicker, and watch the Alastair Sim *Christmas Carol* on television. The great moment was when all five of us spoke, along with Sim, the immortal line, "Are there no prisons? *No workhouses?*"

On Christmas Day we bundled into the car for the larger, dynastic festival at my Aunt Agnes' in Connecticut. Some four generations made a day of it, with drinks and little meatballs at noon as the various cars pulled in, followed by the dread ritual of the Kissing of the Grandparents, the kids trundled into the living room where the old folks stiffly held court in high-backed chairs, my grandfather passing out antique silver dollars to all the dutiful children. "Was he good?" Grandfather would ask as my cousin Ellis filed by. "Very good," said my aunt Laura; and Ellis got a coin. "Was she good?" asked Grandfather, as my cousin Ruth came up. "Basically," my aunt Jane answered; a coin for Ruth. Now it's my turn. "Was he good?" my grandfather inquires of mother, who replies, "He's a perfect little monster-child!" I got a coin anyway, as Mother fumed.

The men sat in on the televised football game in the den, the women traded eternal wisdoms here and there through the house, and the kids repaired outside for touch football with something like twenty on each side, ranging in age from five to thirty. Sacred acts were committed, too, as when my cousins would bring their fiancées to meet their engaged in-laws. I can remember Ellis introducing Sally, person by person, as they moved through the house. Years before, when we were still kids, that time was claimed by the annual Monopoly game, with Ellis, Donald, Jeff, and I behind locked doors as my little brothers and cousins plotted raids outside in the hall. (Ruth still claims she can never forgive us for leaving her out.) Some years, there was a free-for-all upstairs on the third floor, more modern than the rest of the house and amply supplied with huge closets and magical attics. It was the best kind of game: no rules. Everyone just ran around screaming and hiding.

At length came the holiday dinner, in three seatings because of the crush of people. First seating was desirable if you wanted primary choice of the turkey platter, but the second-seating people would come up and stand behind you, grumbling in hunger. Second seating was more convivial but a little thin on the soufflé potatoes; and third seating, reserved for the drunks, who didn't much care whether they ate or not, was a touch campy, with too many green peas. Then came buffet-style coffee and dessert, of an endless suspense punctuated by us kids, who would ask, "Is it time yet?" every three minutes.

By 7:30 or so it was time: for the presents, enough to fill F. A. O. Schwartz for a year. My Uncle Willy was in the toy business, so his were the best—forts, gas stations, and building sets—but there was a general emphasis on things to play with rather than things to wear. My Uncle Mike would read out the cards through a megaphone—"To Bud from Aunt Jane and Uncle Sonny"—as various grownups clapped and the recipient bellowed out a law-abiding "Thank you!" Everyone leaned over to see what came out of the wrapping, and reactions were not muted. Uncle Willy's toys received ovations from the kids, plus cries of "I want that, too!" while the occasional sweater won oohs from the mothers and boos from the kids.

With so many presentations, fathers had to supervise the packing of the gifts in the big cardboard boxes each car had arrived with; the mean fathers dispossessed you of each item almost immediately, while the neat ones (like mine) let you stockpile your haul in the manner of Fafner. Finally, we would be summoned to the kitchen for ice-cream cones, the youngest of us already changed into pajamas. Then, family by family, the clan would disperse. We Pennsylvanians spent much of the night on the road, from Norwalk down through the Bronx to the George Washington Bridge, all the way through New Jersey, and home to Heavensville, my brother Jim and I up front and the oldest and the two youngest in the back with Mother. We had assigned seats for long trips, so she would know whom she was hitting even in the dark. One of my earliest and most pointless memories is of waking up, dimly and momentarily, whenever we stopped for a toll.

I grew up thinking that everyone had the same Christmas; happy families are alike. Coming to New York after college, I learned to my horror that some families simply traded a minor gift or two after dinner. My Jewish friends confirmed the wondrous rumor that Chanukah is like Christmas but *lasts eight days!* Yet they seemed rather blasé about it, and couldn't match Christians for generational pageant. One companion, shockingly calm, told me his parents were Communists and didn't celebrate anything. Worst of all were those who could claim a true holiday but wouldn't join their families. To me, this was like practicing to be an orphan. The sole advantage in having relatives is to be able to go to a Christmas.

Not long ago, my parents moved to California, where my younger brothers live. Then Uncle Mike died, and Aunt Agnes decided to retire from party-giving. Suddenly I was an orphan like many of my set, placeless on Christmas. As they did, I shrugged when asked what I was doing for the holidays. Inwardly, I worried. What could I do? Sit in my armchair scheming and sulking, I suppose; but I do that all the time. The meanest bit of the deal was that I had agreed to mind the Pazuzu-like Bauhaus while Little Kiwi and Dennis Savage were away.

I dropped in as they were packing for their respective trips, Little Kiwi to his folks in Cleveland and Dennis Savage to his sister's in Buffalo.

"Don't forget to give Bauhaus something super for Christmas," Little Kiwi told me.

"He'll be lucky if I fill his water dish."

"If you really wanted to," said Dennis Savage, "you could get a nice party together. Carlo, Lionel, Alex. Don't jive at us just because we've got homes to go to."

"After the Christmases I've known, I'm not going to hunker down with a bunch of overgrown waifs pretending to feel loved."

"Christmas," he says, "is not about love. Christmas is about being with people who are so used to you they take everything you do for granted."

"*You* could have that at the Ramrod."

"Oh? And where could you have that, may I ask?"

Nowhere. My Christmas had vanished: moved away, passed on, grown old. Had it even been available, it could only play as a nostalgic forgery, for touch football and toys have lost their magic now that I am the only cousin of age without a spouse and children. Even my juniors have coupled and are staging their own Christmases, in Scarsdale, Chicago,

Des Moines. A bachelor doesn't quite fit into the Christmas I was raised on. Christmas is about families.

And so, as Dennis Savage and Little Kiwi bustled about, I began to tell them of my Christmas. As I spoke I realized that, yes, everyone does take everyone else for granted: as part of his heritage and destiny. Christmas is the one time of the year when you look about and *feel* your blood. Your race passes before you, epic in little—for instance when my tiniest cousins run up to dance when I play the piano as the grownups dote and clap, or in the spaces left by those departed, very much sensed and even mentioned, almost alive. And there is film on this. I have seen myself at the age of two-and-a-half, from the back, walking up Agnes' tiled pathway in my camel's hair coat, my cousin Donald throwing a welcoming football at my father, my mother sharing a fast confidence with Laura. The camera turns to our car as my father demonstrates the convertible top, hot stuff in those days. Suddenly I turn around for the first time and lo, I'm wearing a Flub-a-Dub mask. Who was holding that camera, Federico Fellini?

"You know," said Dennis Savage, as I subsided, "sometimes your family sounds like *The Forsyte Saga* and sometimes it sounds like *Tobacco Road*."

"Well, your family sounds like *Attack of the Killer Macadamia Nuts*."

"Will you two stop?" cried Little Kiwi, pulling closed the zipper of his valise. "I know you're only fighting because you're both cut off from your brothers."

"Oh yeah?" I countered. "And what do you fight with?"

"I don't fight at Christmas."

"Anyway," said Dennis Savage, "we're packed."

I saw them downstairs to Third Avenue to get a cab, holding Bauhaus on his leash with one hand and a bag of his foodstuffs with the other.

"How cute of you," I noted, "to book simultaneous reservations on different planes."

"It's not cute," said Dennis Savage. "It's expert planning—which, I might add, would have saved you from the terrible curse of Lonely Christmas."

"We're going to have lunch at the airport!" Little Kiwi crowed.

"Hey," I said, "it's snowing."

"A white Christmas!" Little Kiwi breathed.

"Go home," I suggested, between my teeth.

"Don't be sad," said Dennis Savage. "I'll be back in two days."

As they rolled away, Bauhaus looked after them, looked up at me, and began to growl.

"Don't you start in, Buster," I told him.

It was Christmas Eve. Living in midtown, I observe New York's rhapsody of population more than many do, and I saw the crowds, as Robinson Crusoe saw the sea, when I stepped outside for a walk at nightfall. Shoppers, walkers, workers, cranks—the drawbacks of a Christmas lived on the blade. In the Village, Christmas is a rumor, in Brooklyn something done in dark alleys, in the suburbs an arcane rite shut away behind closed doors. But at Fifty-third and Third it's Manhattan at its most dense and fierce. I saw a dumpy little man loaded with wrapped boxes take a cab from a smartly dressed woman who socked him; and when he got into the cab without responding, she spat at him through the open window. A few feet away, two construction workers were trying to help an old man who had fallen, but he was afraid to rise. Behind me, a man in a suit was chasing a hustler, and the boy dashed past us as the man called out, "You'll come back sometime!" He seemed jolly. As I turned away a photographer in leather pants and a knitted cap snapped my picture and ran off. Too bad I wasn't wearing my Flub-a-Dub mask.

It was very cold. I felt like turning back, but I wasn't going to let Christmas spoil *my* holiday. I tried to whirl through the streets, but the crowds held me back, and the noise of the town, too, was heavy, from street musicians to the carol of shattering glass. The last straw was the eruption of Guy Webster out of Brooks Brothers, a dead-on meet, no escape. He wrung my hand and said that, as I was the smartest man in the world, I could save his life by helping him out of a terrible scrape, and, as I was his best friend in the world, I had to. I was thinking that the only thing worse than meeting Guy Webster was meeting Guy Webster's inevitable comrade, Claudia Luxemburg, when Guy added, "And Claudia's here, too!"

Now Guy, I must tell you, is the richest man I know. It's family money, of course: the people I consort with make salaries, not fortunes. Guy and I were in the same class in Friends Academy, and, though we were not chums, we kept bumping into each other later in New York and struck up a sort of acquaintance. I think Guy was fascinated by my independence, for he was very much subject to parental guidance. I know I was fascinated by his *bon ton* set, for at the time I entertained thoughts of becoming a society satirist and hoped to collect material. I gave up early on, after divining that the rich have no emotions. They have manners, they don't litter, and they're apt pretenders at all kinds of skills from boating to sympathizing. A few of them even have style—irony, anyway. But they cannot truly be said to be people, because there just isn't anything they want. However, I could not shake Guy, even when his lofty imperturbility began to get on my nerves and I became crabby with him. In some strangely endearing way he looked up to me—for advice, it seemed, but more exactly for gay glamour, for Guy was semi-closeted and knew neither clones nor queens.

What Guy knew was Claudia. Now, Claudia was what we in the trade call a *fag hag*. This is an almost unusably diffuse term, like "salesman" or "Spaniard" denoting a wide range of characters. Straights seem to think that fag hags are lesbians. No, never. Lesbians are lesbians. Fag hags are straight women who pal around with gay men. No one knows why. Some of them may fear the sexual competition of other women, or the sexual aggression of straight men. Some of them share the gay's whimsically bizarre sense of humor and love of savage elegance and have deserted the straight world as boring. Some of them fall into gay company professionally, through connections in show biz or fashion. Some of them aren't properly of the genre at all, only seem so momentarily—like Helen, my Fire Island hostess, who is something of a genre herself. No two hags are alike, but the bitter term itself suggests the gay's ambivalence—and let's admit that the classic pre-Stonewall hag tended to be a rather unappealing sort, as disgusted by gays as intrigued by them. They hugged the more unappealing men, who would say—after the hag had gotten drunk and offended everyone in the room—"Isn't she *heaven?*"

Guy never said this of Claudia. Guy never said anything that couldn't be uttered resonantly at high noon in the bar of the Piping Rock Club. Claudia never said anything that could; she spoke but one language, High-Middle Cabaret. She was pretty and vivacious, and, in spasms, great fun. But anyone who can spend three hours in a piano bar and meet a request to leave with the statement that "We've just gotten started!" is not my idea of a companion. To top it off, Claudia was unreliable. She had no awareness of time or responsibility, and that drives me wild. Some people show up three hours late for dinner; Claudia would show up a year and three hours late. I can forgive almost nothing, but recklessness especially infuriates me. Yet reckless people somehow gravitate toward me, as if seeking the reproaches their parents spared. Sometimes I feel like every spoiled kid's surrogate father. "Lower your voice," I order Christopher in a bookstore, when he loudly eructates publishing innuendo. "People are starving in China!" I snarl at Little Kiwi, when he throws out leftover food. (He just says, "Oh." When I was young, we told my mother, "So send it to China.")

Claudia's tactless sense of obligation never offended Guy, because the rich don't have much sense of it themselves. There's nowhere that they have to be, ever, nothing that can't be delayed. And Claudia was useful. She gave Guy a feeling for gay without his having to be there in person, and she could show up on his arm when he needed a date. Claudia was what is known as Guy's beard.

"The writer!" Claudia cried, as husbands and wives poured out of Brooks Brothers, their gift lists fulfilled and the hearth beckoning. "Will he help us?"

"Of course he will. He has nothing else to do. Right, Bud?"

"It just so happens," I intoned, "that—"

"Guy," Claudia said, "I'd *kill* for a wee drinkie."

"It just so happens," said Guy, "that anyone alone on the street at this hour is a homeless Christmas bachelor. Now be good and come along and we'll tell you about it."

"Come along where?"

"What's near?" He thought. "The Varsity House."

"They don't have menus," Claudia enthused, as we walked. "You ask for whatever you want and they bring it."

I want my family back, I was thinking; but at least I was in on an adventure. The Varsity House, two blocks northeast of Brooks Brothers—the rich walk, but not far—is one of those places you know, rather than read about. It is nondescript, low-key, virtually hidden behind an unmarked door, and gives the impression that, if your parents didn't come here when they were dating adolescents, your business isn't welcome. The staff greeted Guy by name, and I was relieved to see that I wasn't the only man in a sweater: which reminds us that the rich don't dress up as often as you'd think. Claudia asked for a Scotch with lots of ice and a shrimp cocktail, Guy for scrambled eggs and canteloupe, and I ordered French toast, one of the things a place like this does really well. The rich eat anything they feel like at any time of day, even Cream of Wheat for dinner, if they so choose. Then you ask for seconds on dessert and they look as if they had caught you cadging your dinner out of a garbage can.

Saving Guy's life, it turned out, was simple: I had only to accompany him and Claudia to his parents' traditional Christmas Eve bash.

"Why?"

"Old man," said Guy, "you know how parents are. They *will* ask such-and-such, you know, and I keep fending them off. But now that I'm past thirty . . . well, all this evasion begins to seem ever so slightly tutti-frutti, doesn't it?"

"Why don't you just tell them that such-and-such in men past thirty means that they're. . . ." Guy died in a look, though I was speaking very quietly. "Why don't you tell them that 'bachelor' is a euphemism?"

"My dear fellow alumnus, they'd raving *shoot* me."

"I remember your parents. They seemed rather sweet."

"Well, they are sweet. They just think these incredibly grave thoughts about renouncing and disinheriting. My boy, it's like an opera. Anyway, my back is against the wall at last, so I told them I'd bring my sweetheart along tonight. I *told* them. 'My sweetheart.' The exact words."

"Guess who got the part?" said Claudia, simulating a resumé photograph.

"Where do I fit in?"

He patted my hand. "Imagine."

"Can't." Rich people think it's dashing when you leave out the subject pronouns.

"Well . . . my sweetheart Claudia and I can't face it alone, is the thing."

"He can't face it," said Claudia. "I sense it's high time I made my debut. And had another wee drinkie."

"They've never met her, you know. My parents." In this place, you simply point to a glass and a waiter refills it. Guy pointed; a wee drinkie for Claudia. "And if there were a group of us, I was thinking . . . well, just saying to Claudia, in fact. If there were someone we could *call* . . . and you came along like the cavalry. I mean, look: fellow schoolchum, old boy network, author and man-about-town, aunts and uncles gather 'round to worship, parents impressed . . . You can take the pressure off Claudia and me."

"I don't want to spend Christmas being your ruse," I

141

said. "And I'm not a man-about-town and I *don't* approve of closet cover procedures."

"Jeepers, man, must I sing 'The Red and Black Fight Song'?" This was Friends Academy's football anthem, the stirring performance of which before each game seemed to guarantee our stupendous defeat, though we probably would have lost, anyway. At least we played. When the wrestling team stood challenge to a public school, we sometimes defaulted matches because one of our side refused to go to the mat with a black. "I'll give you my watch. I'll give you my shoes."

"Guy—"

"Anything you want, for heaven's sake!"

"What I want, you cannot give."

"Unlike me," Claudia observed. "I want to star in a revival of *Flora, the Red Menace*. Guy could produce it, like a sugar daddy of the 1920s."

"Don't sing," Guy told her, because she often does, anywhere, loud.

But the sad truth of it was: What else did I have to do?

One thing you must not dare is to enter a rich people's Christmas in less than the higher threading; we repaired to my place so I could change. While Claudia poured herself another wee drinkie, Guy glanced through my closet and silently chose a suit, tie, shirt, and handkerchief. "Black socks and shoes," he concluded.

"I could have done that myself," I said.

"I'm faster."

"This is my fanciest suit," I noted. "Just how heavy is this party, anyway?"

"Well, it's the whole clan, you know. The one time of the year when we're all together. Even Aunt Eliza—and she doesn't come to anything." He put his hand on my shoulder. "It's the command performance, old chap. It's major, is what. So you can see how terribly eager I am to breeze through it, if possible. You see it, don't you?"

142

I took the clothes into the bathroom. "Excuse me for saying so," I whispered, "but aren't your parents counting on your showing up with some debutante? Claudia isn't exactly a Colonial Dame right off the *Arbella*."

"That's her charm." He winked at me. "You aren't planning to wear those dark glasses, are you? Have you any hornrims or something like that?"

"Whoa!"

"Anyway, I don't have to show up with a fiancée, just a date. They simply want to assure themselves that I'm not . . . you know."

"Tutti-frutti."

He giggled. "Actually, Claudia is perfect casting. She's so colorful they won't put me through this again for at least a decade."

I stopped dressing and looked at him.

"But lest she overwhelm the place," he went on, "you can lend our company an air of . . . well . . ."

"*Zoom!*" said Claudia, edging in with her wee drinkie. "I want to zoom all over, like Liza in 'Mein Herr.' Can I go in dark glasses, too?"

We compromised on the glasses: I wore none at all, which makes me dangerously liable to nearsighted acts such as trying to charm people who are glaring at me.

The streets were deserted all of a sudden: New York had all gone home. In the cab, Claudia went into a medley of what she called "show biz goldies"—mostly *Carousel* cut with *On Your Toes*—but broke off when she took in the depth of the gathering snowfall and breezed into "White Christmas."

"Come on," she urged. "Somebody on harmony."

"It would be funny," I said, "if after all this I did something embarrassing at the party."

Guy turned a bland smile on me, which read, Anyone who went to school with Guy Webster is a perfect gentleman.

Traffic was moving so slowly that Claudia had time not only to put us through "White Christmas" but to drill us in descants and festive effects, such as adding "and emerald" between the two words of the title and having the men impose a descending chromatic line over the melody on "May your days be merry and bright." It sounded ragged but sweet, and I caught the taxi driver furtively joining in. Through it all, I was distracted by the humming of the meter, but Guy was perfectly at ease, as are all rich people when they hear money being spent, including their own. I don't mean just anyone with money, mind you, but the *genetically* rich, those born to a culture of largesse—a culture as textured and developed as the gay system is. One Christmas in my youth, I was given a cocker spaniel puppy who was so excited to be out of the kennel that he couldn't settle down and go to sleep, so my mother put a clock in his basket and the ticking soothed him. So it is, I believe, with the rich and taxi meters.

"Next could we do 'Good Christian Men, Rejoice'?" said the taxi driver.

"We only do Broadway-type carols," said Claudia.

"On the right, driver," said Guy. "Fourth house along."

It was literally a house: the Websters lived in the whole thing. The front door alone warned you that the building was like a human bank: an immensely thick bar of glass protected fore and aft by elaborate iron webbing. The man who opened the door actually called our host Mr. Guy, which gave Claudia the idea of going as Miss Glama de Ponselle.

"Claudia," Guy said, "things are touchy enough as it is."

"Miss Glama," she insisted, "is ready for her wee drinkie. Miss Glama de Ponselle."

"Guy!" cried a handsome man in the most beautifully tailored dinner clothes I've ever seen, sailing down the stairs. "Well, egad, old son!" They shook hands, and Guy introduced him as Cousin Brian. Another thing about the rich is that the men are usually good-looking but not sexy.

"And I'm Miss Glama," said Claudia, before Guy could say she wasn't. "Believe me, one day when I'm a celeb, you'll wish you knew me."

"I wish I knew you now," Brian answered, amused.

"Did Aunt Eliza make it?"

144

"Everyone's here, and there's a heavy air of Santa in the air. Come along, lad. Now is the time for the good little boys to claim their reward."

I bet it's somewhat more than a dollar, too, I said to myself as we ascended. Aunt Agnes' was never like this Christmas. True, there were the seniors sedately postured, the aunts and uncles grouped, the little kids in cute little versions of grown-up clothes racing around deliriously. But there was none of the sit-back-and-dish atmosphere that my aunts observed, none of my uncles' hearty thunder. There were no decorations, no presents, no bowls of pretzels. Surely no Monopoly game was in session down the hall. There were waiters wafting about with trays of fancy food that no one named Webster had cooked, little groups of people nodding to each other, and even the pianist noodling show tunes was clearly a hired man, not some obliging nephew.

"Piano bar!" Claudia breathed.

"Miss Havisham," I murmured, viewing a tremendous crone in a stupendous chair bearing a fabulous cane. Other family types posed behind her like lawyers at a board meeting.

"That's Aunt Eliza," said Guy.

"Claudia and I will scatter to the bar," I offered.

"No," said Guy, clutching us. "This is central."

"Guy," Aunt Eliza wheezed, as we approached. "Guy," she added, as he kissed her cheek. "Guy," she concluded, pounding her cane. "Do you smoke?"

"No, ma'am."

"Do you drink?"

"Sometimes."

"That's a good boy. That's a man. I hate a smoker, or a pantywaist who doesn't know his whiskey." She eyed Claudia, who curtsied as to royal majesty. "Lovely, child." Aunt Eliza proposed the kissing of her sere cheek, and Claudia managed nicely. "Whose is she? Ellen's? Is it Ellen's girl?"

"No, Aunt Eliza, this is my friend—"

"Miss Glama de Ponselle."

Aunt Eliza listened to the name as one attends agitated noises in the hall outside one's apartment door. "I sense New Orleans or such."

"Boston."

The old bag brightened. "Ah."

Now I was dragged forward, introduced as a writer.

"I love Dickens," Aunt Eliza declared, not to my surprise. "Are you Dickensian?"

"Sometimes," I said, as Little Nell, Smike, and Sidney Carton shrieked in their graves. "With a modern edge."

"Rubbish!" Aunt Eliza remarked. "Guy, you will appear before me later. I've something to give you."

"Yes, ma'am."

Having earned our dollars, we slipped over to the bar as Guy greeted his family.

"I know the pianist," Claudia told me. "He plays at Carstair's."

"Do you people hire out?" said Brian, coming up. "Guy's not the only one who needs support at parties."

"The writer's all booked up with Dickensian novels," said Claudia. "But I'm possible."

Brian smiled. Great teeth, and surprisingly broad shoulders for a rich boy. At Guy's signal, I excused myself, crossed the floor, dodged two adorable little girls imitating robots and screaming "Wind me up! Wind me up!" and found myself facing Guy's parents.

There are two kinds of rich parents. The men are either Ichabod Crane or Franklin Roosevelt and the women are Eleanor Roosevelt or Queen Elizabeth II. Guy had FDR and the Queen. Stunning; and they had this way of speaking so profoundly about such trivia that after two minutes with them you'd be ready to best Henry James at parlor banter.

"Layered," was all I said to Guy as we moved on. "Heavily layered."

"He published seven of the ten most imposing novels of the early 1950s and she opened the first surrealist gallery in

146

New York. They should have had you for a son. Now it's Claudia's turn."

"Do you know Glama sings?" said Brian, joining us. "At this very moment she's—"

"Oh, my gosh," Guy whispered, turning to the piano.

"You," Claudia was singing, very freely, "do," with her hands folded together, "something to me." The pianist swung gracefully into rhythm, Claudia's hands opened, and the guests gathered round as Miss Glama launched her vaudeville.

Brian told Guy, "You have gifted friends."

The odd thing was, Claudia was good. Hags who take over at the piano usually try to jazz up "Mister Snow" or tack a cakewalk finale onto "My Heart Stood Still." Claudia did not overplay, or blow lyrics, or go flat. She sounded like a pro doing a gig. She and the pianist were so in tune that on the second chorus they jumped the key a whole step without signaling to each other; something in her voice warned him and he followed. There was applause and, after scarcely a second's whisper, the pianist struck up "The Physician," Cole Porter's number about the doctor whose interest in his patient is strictly physical. It's what used to be called "naughty": wittily suggestive if you're worldly but shockingly doubly-meant if you aren't. I wondered how Aunt Eliza might take it. She was oblivious, busy with her inquisition; and those of the guests who were listening seemed appreciative.

"'But he never said he loved me,'" Claudia sang.

"Is she in the theatre?" Brian asked me.

"I believe so, yes."

"She's a brick. You so often hear this song camped about, don't you? But she's ace with it. Fresh." I was surprised to hear this knowledgeable commentary, but then I reminded myself that rich people often know about Cole Porter, because he was One of Them: rich. On the other hand, he was also One of Us: gay. Just then, Guy's father asked if he could speak to me upstairs.

I toyed with asking, "Why?" One advantage in attending rich people's parties is you can get away with anything, though of course they may not ask you back, which is their idea of punishment. But I was here as Guy's diplomat, and felt bound to "suave it out," as Little Kiwi has taken to putting it.

"'But he never said he loved *me*,'" Claudia sang, as I affably accompanied Mr. Webster up another rolling stairway into a room of leather and wood, books and prints—and, astonishingly, an old wind-up Victrola, which instantly gave us something friendly to explore. As every aficionado does, Mr. Webster pulled out treasures to delight me, and, as the disks spun and the uniquely reverberant sounds poured out, I thought of my late grandmother, an unlovably eccentric but fiercely musical woman who introduced me to 78s. Her taste was much like Mr. Webster's: symphony, opera, show music, and dance-band pop. As he retrieved Victor Herbert's recording of his "March of the Toys" from the turntable, Mr. Webster said, "I feel it important to tell you that Mrs. Webster and myself are relieved."

"Relieved?"

"That Guy has finally been honest with us." He said this mildly, as he said everything. "He may have wanted to protect us by keeping his . . . well, his love life . . . secret. But I don't think it truly serves a family to be too discreet. There is such a thing as intimacy, isn't there?"

"Surely."

He put no more records on, so this was what he had wanted to speak of. But why to me?

"I expect it is premature to say so, but I think Guy has done well for himself. I confess, I really wasn't sure what . . . sort of person, if I may say so, we were to encounter."

"Ah."

"Guy tells me you went to Friends Academy together."

"Yes."

"I always think it best when two people share a background. It makes the routine things so much easier." He smiled. "As opposed to the notorious *nostalgie de la boue,* if you'll pardon my boldness."

Suddenly I had the impression that I was missing something. Not as much as I would have been missing if he had been speaking, say, entirely in Lithuanian, but something at the core of the topic.

"How long," he then said, "have you and Guy been lovers?"

That's what I had been missing.

"I will respect your silence," he went on, "if you would rather not speak of this."

I tried to collect my thoughts.

"Do you, like me, speak Lithuanian?"

No, he didn't say that—yet he might as well have done, given the flow of conversation. As so often with closeted scions, the parents were better informed than had been supposed. Well, what do you do when the father of your friend says he likes your friend's taste in romance, as opposed to the hard-hat or trucker he might have chosen if *nostalgie de la boue* had won out? I was still speechless, momentarily bemused by the picture of the meticulous Guy seeking something hot from the underworld. Guy's idea of rough trade is a Raggedy Andy doll.

I had to say something. "Who," I said, "is that masked man?"

"I beg your pardon?"

"My family gives a party like this, though rather more informally. Or we used to give them. And like other Americans we took movies. You know those old home color reels, that you'd send to Rochester in those yellow boxes?"

He nodded, intrigued.

"Well, my parents moved to California not long ago, and before they left we hauled out the films and ran them one last time in the east. There's one of me, at the Christmas party, in a Flub-a-Dub mask. And the strange thing is, I didn't just wear that mask for the movie. I wore it all day, from meatballs to ice cream, no matter what anyone said."

"But what is a Flub-a-Dub?"

"The Flub-a-Dub was a character on the Howdy Doody Show. Grotesque, animalistic, and illiterate. His act consisted of mixing up words."

If Mr. Webster was a publisher, he would know a theme when he heard one outlined.

"A rather piquant choice of alter ego for a writer," he observed.

"Well, I'm not illiterate. But I do mix up words, in a way. And the mask is the essential image, not the character."

"The mask?"

I nodded. "I am the masked man."

He thought. "But you were not . . . forgive me—not hired, surely?"

"I was beseeched."

"I see."

"Guy's got a mask on, too. And he'll probably be glad to take his off. If you tell him you know, and that it's all right. . . ."

He considered this solemnly, then slowly unfolded a Mona Lisa smile. "I believe I thought I *had* told him."

"In those words?"

"I don't suppose one ever does anything in precisely the words. You make it sound ingeniously simple. Was it like that with your parents?"

"My parents," I said, "are too attached to their children to let the luck of the draw cause trouble among us."

He thought this over, slowly winding up the record player. "Then," he announced at length, "I will play you one last side, and no pun is intended." It was Fanny Brice's "Cooking Breakfast for the One I Love." Superb. And downstairs we then went.

Claudia was on break, a wee drinkie in her hand, Guy and Brian flanking her.

"How can you not be sozzled by this time?" I asked her. "All those drinkies."

150

"Oh, they're mostly ice," she said. "And I never finish them. Drinking is entirely a matter of style."

"We have to talk," said Guy—but his father, Mrs. Webster attending, was pointing to him the way Guy had pointed to Claudia's glass in The Varsity House. Whatever you want, the rich are taught from infancy, just point to it.

Gazing about me, I thought, This is the ultimate completion of the Christmas bachelor: to sanction the festivities of strangers. I hate party small talk. I hate food cut into tiny strips on silver dollars of white bread. I hate being served. I hate Aunt Eliza. How is one to feel his blood at such a party? You believe in the Christmas you were raised on; you cannot cross over.

"What did you tell him?" Guy asked me, a bit later, when he returned from upstairs. "Egad, they're . . . *happy!*"

"I didn't tell him anything," I replied. "They already knew."

"Knew what?" asked Claudia.

"That the world is full of masked men," I replied.

Now we were all summoned to the elders' part of the party, where the presents were to be distributed. There were no forts or gas stations, no megaphone, no Uncle Mike. There weren't even packages. It was all envelopes, even for the littlest kids; and thank yous were not hurled out but solemnly nodded. One gift put a stutter into this ceremonial rhythm, when Aunt Eliza pulled out a battered jewelry box of the kind that Edwin Drood might have kept his collar studs in. She opened it, gazed upon its contents, slowly extracted an antique watch, and said, "Come here, Guy."

He came.

"This was Grandfather's," said Aunt Eliza, her voice cracking. "You must have it now."

Hums and murmurs.

"It has tradition on this Christmas day," she went on. "It has a meaning in the family. And that is the most important thing to have."

There should be film on this, I thought. Too bad there

were no cameras about. Cameras and masks and watches, a Christmas!

Aunt Eliza handed the watch to Guy and commemorated the presentation with a crash of her cane. Everyone clapped.

"There are four of those watches in the world," Brian whispered to Claudia and me. "One for each of my great-great-grand-uncles. Three have been passed on, so this is the last of the group."

The casing was silver, elaborately chased, the inner surface inscribed with a name and date, the piece itself extraordinary. That's one thing rich people are good for: amazing presents.

They are also good for inviting you out to the Brasserie for some real food on plates, which Brian did after Claudia had sung another set and Aunt Eliza had raged at a minor cousin who had had the temerity to challenge her politics. I could almost hear her roaring, "Are there no prisons? *No workhouses?*"

We were all somewhat carefree as we paraded downstairs to get our coats, and on the far side of merry by the time we had reached the restaurant and made the first toast, to Aunt Eliza's cane. Brian was a grand host; without imploring or condescending, he made you know that he would feel disappointed if you didn't go for it and order something really spiffy.

I was jovial. Guy was utterly on top of the town, for the only serious problem in his life had been solved: his folks now knew of and proposed to live with his sexuality. And Claudia was shining, with three straight men playing to her—Brian in the literal sense, Guy in the Pickwickian sense, and I in the vaudevillian sense. True enough, she didn't really imbibe, just held. The rest of us, however, drank champagne, and Brian kept it coming. We men had reached that level of sauced euphoria in which we are still physically presentable but our mouths are blurting out confidences.

"This is the one, true Christmas," I heard myself say.

"Really. Consider its parts: relatives, champagne, presents, the Kissing of the Grandparents—"

"You didn't get a present," said Guy.

I shrugged happily.

After Brian excused himself, Claudia announced that she was up for a present that night.

"What?"

"Your cousin."

"Take care, Claudia," said Guy. "Brian's something of a womanizer, you know."

"Oh, that's my favorite kind," she replied. "What's a womanizer?"

"A straight Lothario," I explained.

"I'm in the nude," Claudia sang, "for love . . ."

Guy suddenly said, "You know what they told me?"

"'We still love you,'" I guessed.

"How did you know?"

"They always say that. The nice ones."

"A writer," said Claudia, "knows all the stories."

"Did you ever hear about the gay bachelor on Christmas Eve?" I asked.

"Do tell," said Claudia.

"He learns that if you can't spend Christmas with your family, then you have an adventure."

"That's good to know," said Claudia, "but the important thing is, you look so much better without those dark glasses."

"That may well be," said Guy. "I lost mine tonight, too."

"How does it feel?"

"Sporty."

Claudia raised a glass. "Christmas, love, and peace, fellow gypsies." We clinked and drank. "Now each of us make a wish for the new year."

"Mumps to my enemies," I said.

"No cab strikes," said Guy. "Claudia?"

"No more world hunger and an especially zoomy revival of *Mack and Mabel* with me as Mabel."

"That's two wishes," said Brian, rejoining us. "And who's Claudia?"

"What would you ask for?" she said.

He flashed a Piping Rock smile at her. "I like everything as it is."

That's the rich for you.

Outside the restaurant, we broke into couples, Claudia and Brian waiting for the correct moment in which to hail a cab and Guy and I doing that bashful, recapitulatory ceremony typical of gays who have shared an intimate experience yet do not really know each other. Rather than talk about ourselves, we admired the geography, Manhattan's great stupas lighting the snowfall, the towers concealed in a brilliant mist, the vision a rhetoric of power and daring and elitism. These are the principles of Manhattan capitalism, and its setting that night was an electro-industrial Switzerland, virtually a natural wonder. And we belong to it, and own it.

From a few feet off, the sounds of "White Christmas" floated over to us, Brian gamely holding the descant on "May your days be merry and bright." When we turned to see, they were kissing, and Guy and I shook hands like foxy grandpas.

Off the lovers went, and I walked Guy to Third Avenue before we, too, parted. We talked a bit more, aimlessly, then he put his hand in the pocket of my overcoat.

"This is a present," he said. "Don't take it out till you get home. Okay?"

"But I have nothing for you."

I started to put my hand in my pocket, but he stopped me. "I demand," he said, trying to cow me with his generations. "You already gave me mine."

He pointed at a cab and it skidded over. I watched him pull away, and waved; but the rich seldom look back.

The first thing I did when I got home was to take Bauhaus out for his walk, the second to call my parents, the third to light up a pipe, and the fourth to pull Guy's present out of my coat. It was a silver pocket watch, the inside of the cover reading, "Ch.<u>S</u> Tuyler Webster, 1878."

"He must have been drunk!" Dennis Savage cried when I showed him. "You got him drunk and palmed his watch! You probably get your bed partners that way, too!"

"You ought to know."

"Of course you'll return it!"

"Of course," I agreed, thinking that could take years.

"Besides robbing the rich and starving Bauhaus, not that he doesn't deserve it, what else have you been up to while I was gone?"

"I've been writing up my Christmas adventure!"

"Branching out into science-fiction?"

"It just so happens, Mister Smarty, that I spent Christmas holding a family together, and teaching a closeted gay to have confidence in himself, and setting up a very cute straight couple. What did you do, may I ask? Add to your sister's already legendary Tupperware collection and try to lure your brother-in-law into wrestling matches. What's more, I'm writing a Dickensian story about it, with, I must admit, a modern edge. What have you written lately? And I have learned what place an orphan may take in the Christmas pageant, and that a bachelor may luxuriate in Christmas spirit as surely as any family man. After all, I can't go to Aunt Agnes' for the rest of my life. I can love tradition in other ways. Yea, I can undergo the rites. You think not? You are a benighted queen. I can give and be given to. And, by the way, contrary to what you believe, it turns out that Christmas is about love, after all. The name is love. And I have learned all this, and you have learned—and in any case know—nothing. So what do you have to say to that, you soigné debutante?"

He sat down, crossed his legs, and smiled. He mimed lighting a cigarette, puffing, exhaling. He smiled again. "You know what you aren't?" he said. "New wave."

The Disappearance of
Roger Ryder

Gay life has not only its episodic naturalism—its true stories—but its mythology, too. On those nights out at the Pines when heavy rain prohibits a walk to the dance hall and a table cluttered with dinner things reproaches the slightest attempt to Do Something, one of us will recount a legend or two, perhaps that of the most intense man in New York, or the most handsome, or the most betrayed, or the most bizarre.

I prefer the tale of the most disguised man, the one who got to . . . well, listen and judge for yourself what he got. I have told this tale on many a night on the beach, sometimes including my listeners in the action. They may resent this, or laugh nervously, but they attend: for we are in these fantasies as surely as we are in our biographies.

I start with the unemployed actor Roger Ryder, standing on sand in the late afternoon, alone. The straight sweep of the beach, countless miles in either direction, is empty, as the code of the Pines recommends. Everyone else is housed and waiting. There will be tea, dinner, startling recreations: the summer begins.

Roger paces, carrying a Scotch and dying a little faster than the rest of us, because hope is an oik jeering in the gallery. Most actors arrive on some level by the time they're twenty-eight, a minority come through in their early thirties, and a very few squeak by later through fluke or some unspeakable arrangement. All the others—most actors, in truth—wake up at the age of forty to realize that they have scarcely been actors at all. They are waiters or word processors and will never be anything else. Roger, thirty-three-and-a-half, worries more than he hopes.

Once in a while a runner flashes by along the edge of the surf, a pure image of sport, boldness, health. What is their motivation? How would one portray a runner? Have they a rapt childhood, a contentious vocation, a favorite pie? Roger is up for a part in a soap—not a great part, nor yet a great soap. Still, in Roger's profession they say "Everything is potential." Given the right space, the right text, and the right lighting, you can be anything. Roger has played a dragon, a Chinese conjuror, a crazed vegetarian—even Hamlet, in Louisville, where it doesn't count. The dragon, in the second-grade Christmas pageant, was his greatest role; through perverse, cocky ad libs, he made such a hit that he was elected class president for the next three years. Things have slowed up somewhat since, and now there's Roger waiting for a break. Sometimes he tries to will something to happen.

How foolish, the Pines, to abandon the beach when it is most enchanting. By day what a dire festival, as competitive as an Olympic stadium; now, open and accessible under its darkening sun, it is serenely epic. The runners pass through as if anywhere were more useful than here, yet they always come back, their faces as concentratedly thoughtless as before. Who are they? Accountants, physicists, spies? *Waiters?* A man in running shorts tells you nothing.

Another man is walking the beach, about fifteen houses to the west. Black Speedos. Another runner probably, set for the gainless race. Roger sips his drink and admires the sea. Wednesday he has his soap interview; a reading too, if they like him. They might. It's one of those protean best-friend parts they plop in during a lull, to test viewer response before energizing the character with romantic commotion. Trouble is, they never warn you how to present yourself: what to act. They don't tell you because they don't know. They look and they listen. Maybe you hit them right; maybe you don't.

The man in black Speedos isn't heading for the wet sand

157

where the runners live. He prowls the dunes, like Roger, but not aimlessly, like Roger. As he nears, he breaks into outline: black hair and moustache, broad shoulders, spacious torso, trim waist. Tall and strong, with a take-no-prisoners air. Perhaps on his way to cocktails at the east end of the Pines, where the big money is. One of those parties in which fat garment center honchos audition houseboy talent.

Another sip of Scotch and Roger ambles toward the ocean, pondering Wednesday's choices. What do you project when no one knows who you're supposed to be? The brisk man? The ebullient kid? Sloppy grin, wanton eyes? Keen patter? Or silence? The less you give the more they want.

Give me a hit, Roger thinks, and I'd own this beach. I know how to use power. Especially here—the most sophisticated village in the world acting like the most primitive. It could be a Greek city–state of two or three millennia ago, waiting out a cultural intermission till the next god comes. Thebes, maybe. Thebes awaiting the next god. Turning to the line of houses above the dunes to raise his glass in toast, Roger sees the stranger in black Speedos, forty feet away and heading right toward him. My God, what a stunning man— no, *shockingly* beautiful!

"What's your wish?" he asks Roger.

"I'll bet you've heard this before, but if your smile isn't outlawed, I can't be held responsible for any consequent collapse of civil order."

"Nay, the collapse of order is what I plan."

"Nay?" Roger smiles.

"You must help." The stranger grasps Roger by the shoulders.

"Anything, to put it mildly."

"I've formed a gang. We'd like to tap you."

"Tap me?"

"For the gang."

"I thought 'tap' might be new Castro argot."

"If you join, you get to take any form you like. Physically. *Any form.* You change at will, every detail to your

158

order. The professional advantages alone would be decisive. And socially, the possibilities are infinite, are they not?"

"Could I have my shoulders back?"

The stranger strokes Roger's hair.

"I don't know what you're on," Roger says, "but where can I get some?"

"Join us," the stranger urges. "You might be the thousand most handsome men alive. That would be worth . . . what? A million within three years. And our revenge program guarantees atrocious deaths to all your enemies. Have you enemies?"

"Just my agent."

The shoulders again. "I would be so glad to collect you, young fellow."

"Your place or mine?"

The stranger turns Roger to face the houses, holding him from behind. "So much. Look. You can encircle it. Look. Every day there's more. In a thousand years you couldn't exhaust the supply. And you'll have that long. Imagine. Taste it. Look."

"I love this."

The stranger smooths Roger's cheek. "So many possibilities!"

"You're wonderful. Who are you?"

"*You can change your looks*. Is there a greater gift?"

Roger pulls away. "Listen, ace, are you taking me home or not?"

"I offer you the world and you fasten on one! Use the head, young fellow: if you join my gang, you'll never need anyone again. You'll have it all. If the world is full of splendid men, can one be unique?"

"Okay, okay." Roger's eyes rake the houses. "Okay, whose idea was this? My entire house is on somebody's deck, watching through binoculars, right? Let's send the most gorgeous man in the Pines out to Roger and watch him get stirred up. It'll pass the time till tea. Well, let me tell you, gorgeous is as gorgeous does."

"Hush." The stranger puts his fingers against Roger's lips. "Hush, now." He smiles, and Roger becomes as peaceful as a melted Humorette. "I don't usually have this much trouble."

"I'll just bet you don't."

"Want proof? Where's your drink?"

Roger looks around.

"You had a glass of Scotch when I met you. Where is it now?"

"I must have put it down somewhere."

"Nowhere. We've been standing here the whole time."

Roger laughs. "Poof, you made my drink vanish?"

"Join my gang?"

"Are you going to tell me who you are, or what?"

"I'm the gang leader."

"All right, I'll join. One condition: I want to be initiated by you."

The stranger lets out a low, dirty ratchet-whirl of a laugh, the sole unattractive piece in his kit. "My gang will initiate you."

Roger is silent.

"The deal runs thus. Three months of unconditional transformation privileges, no quota, all types, clothes included. Change as often as you like. When you tire of one look, move on to another, or drop back into your born form as you choose. I ask you only not to take the form of anyone else, living or dead. It gets touchy, and you bring heat down on the gang, and that would make me enormously displeased with you." He very gently rubs Roger's lips with his thumb. "We wouldn't want that, would we?"

Still Roger is silent.

"Would we?"

Roger shakes his head.

"Now, what do you give for three months' free passage in the labyrinth of love?"

"I've been trying to give you my heart for the last half hour."

160

"It's customary for new members to run errands for us after their three months. We find it a pleasant way to instill a sense of gang loyalty. Unconditional loyalty, I need add."

"'Then is doomsday near.'"

"It's very enjoyable work: introducing corporate executives to drugs of pleasure, luring reformed alcoholics back to dreams of drink, making theatre critics cranky just before a Sondheim premiere, tripping nuns . . . a droll life."

"I don't think I'd be good at it."

"You'd be surprised what you'll be good at after three months of feeling the invulnerability of absolute beauty."

"What if I change my mind somewhere up the road?"

"Can't."

"What if I *do?*"

"Then I'll send for Jocko."

"Listen, does your keeper know you're out?"

"Now it begins. They're massing up for tea, and you'll make your debut. Go. Intoxicate them."

"Don't I get a magic kabunga or something? To transform myself with? With dials for face, physique, and points beyond?"

"Young fellow." The stranger rests a heavy hand on Roger's neck. "Your jesting hurts my heart."

"Why don't you come along to tea, anyway? I love walking in with something terrific."

"This day you will." He gives Roger a push. "Go."

Roger takes a few steps, then turns. "Will I see you again?"

"I'll be checking in to follow your progress. And good luck on Wednesday."

Roger comes back. "All right. Whom do you know that I know, and what's this about, really?"

"This is about deception."

"Yes, I see that."

"You've sharp eyes and a good mind. That's why I chose you. Savvy is moribund; and there's no fun in corrupting the dull. My gang is keen as razors."

They face each other for a moment. Roger nods. The stranger nods.

"You know," says Roger. "I . . . I like . . . the way you call me 'young fellow.'"

"That's all right, then. Come." They proceed to the boardwalk. "Do as I say and we'll be close. We'll talk of things, and I'll befriend you. Now go there."

Roger moves on alone. At the stairs leading to the boardwalk, Roger turns. The stranger waves. His grin shines for a mile. Roger climbs to the walk and, at an idle pace, deep in thought, Dionysus enters Thebes.

Actors are vagabond, and Roger Ryder jumped from house to house over the summers, landing at last with old friends in the thorny forest on the bay west of the harbor. They were short one share, and had been entertaining possibilities, thus far without luck. It was a quiet house, preferring dish to radio and chance to rules. The first weekend, someone brought out a gym-and-disco queen who kept house in a cockring and infuriated everyone with his "party tapes," largely strenuous rock spliced into remarks made during torrid encounters. The next weekend, someone else produced an academic whose field was the use of the gerundive in early-middle Millais. It was his only topic of conversation. A quiet house: but this was too quiet. The third weekend brought a live wire, who had the idea that he must win his place through divertissement. Armed with sets of Scrabble and Mille Bornes ("That touch of camp!" he cried; none knew why), trivia quiz books, and barnyard impersonations, he held the house in rumpus till someone slipped a synthetic substance into his Yoo-Hoo, whereupon he organized a variety show and led off with an act of pastiche farting, in the styles of various show biz personalities. Then he passed out. Heading for the Botel, everyone was in a sour mood, because, really, was there no one of minimally acceptable appearance, character, intelligence? Is that asking much?

Tea was tea, changeless: a validation of the eternally renewable fantasy. No backstory compromises the breadth of shoulders, no giggle ridicules the stomach-waist declension, no keening mother or kvetching father humiliates the ambitions of a truly inspiring nipple radius. Mystery, here, is the one honesty, truth in a glance. There is, sure enough, the tactless intimacy of gathered data, when last summer's most spectacular houseboy turns up in something like a dress, or when a man celebrated for decades appears sagging at the belt line. But there is always something new to browse. There is fame; there is notoriety; there is absolute visibility. And the day that Roger Ryder's housemates came fretting out of their cottage, still smoking from the entertainer's fire, someone whirled up out of nowhere and, in an instant, the hundred men present glimpsed, feared, and loved him. "Man of death!" Roger's friend Paul breathed.

Everything was big, pointed, bold. A fairy must have spun his golden hair, a sculptor cut his lines, an alchemist dyed his green eyes, a watchmaker tightened his parts.

He smiled at Paul.

Paul whispered, "He burned my face!"

Fifty men fell silent; the other fifty began to hiss. The blond stood at the top of the entrance stairs and scanned the population. He saw plops wither, clones glumly marvel, contenders defensively flash their best feature, two adorable punks silently whimper, and a smashing muscleman—who had one flaw, a raucous nose—shudder and go slack.

The blond strode to the bar and smiled at the bartender. "Let me have a beer."

The bartender also smiled, and didn't move.

The blond put a hand on the bartender's, caressing the middle finger. "Hey. Hey. How about that beer?"

The bartender stared. "Coming right up." Yet he was still.

"Take your time."

The bartender rummaged in a trance behind the counter. "One . . ."

"Beer."

". . . right . . ."

"Any brand."

". . . and . . ."

"Bottled or canned."

". . . yes . . ."

"Preferably bottled."

The bartender gave him three glasses, seven twists of lime, and a box of napkins. "On the house," he murmured.

"Thank you."

Suddenly awake, the bartender found a can of something. "And the beer, of course." He essayed a laugh.

The blond took another survey of the space. His eye lit upon a dark-haired youth whose cynical, hot-angles face played a fetching contrast with his elegant, hot-curves physique. The youth felt the blond's eye, turned to meet it, looked away, looked back, and held it.

The crowd rustled in wonder.

The blond nodded thoughtfully.

The youth walked up to him.

The crowd tensed.

The youth looked at the blond; the blond leaned over and whispered in his ear. The youth looked down and carefully nudged the edge of the blond's foot with his own.

The crowd moaned.

Locked eye to eye, the blond and the youth left together.

And fifty men turned to the other fifty men and said, "I want to die."

At about nine that night, Paul was checking the lasagna as Albert set to designing the table settings. "Origami napkins!" he decided.

"Penguins," Paul suggested. "Or little dinosaurs."

"If only I knew origami," said Albert.

The entertainer was still passed out.

Franklin got off the phone. "Even Barry Thompson doesn't know who he was. No one has ever seen him before. He's literally unheard of."

164

"Maybe he's Alexander the Great come back."

"Alexander was short."

"But great!"

"Barry says half the Pines has been ringing Wayne Calder's house and no one answers."

"Wayne Calder?"

"The boy he took home."

"Just remember," said Paul. "I'm the one he smiled at."

Roger came in.

"You missed everything!"

"'The players cannot keep counsel,'" Roger replied. "'They'll tell all.'"

"The *most* incredible man—"

"To die!"

"Wearing nothing but—"

"And whispered as if—"

"Stop." Roger peered into the oven. "Oh good, lasagna." He grinned at them. "I happen to know the case."

"Who is he?" They crowded, sat near, posed, twirled. The fun of the Pines!

"Who he is is not clear." Roger poured himself a drink. "But it is told that Wayne Calder wept for happiness as he was being stripped."

"No!"

"Name your source!"

"And, in a dear moment, they tell, Wayne murmured, 'If an officer finds us, we'll be put in the brig for life.'"

"Scream!"

"No!"

"*More!*"

"The question is," said Franklin, "is Wayne Calder beautiful or just sexy?"

"He misses being handsome," said Albert, "but the body is truly historic."

"Here's what I want to know," Paul put in. "What did the mystery man whisper to Wayne before they left?"

165

Roger said, "He whispered, 'I want to lay you on your back and deep-pump you full of joy.'"

Silence.

"The tactless majesty of the beautiful," Roger called it. "They speak their own language."

The conversation eventually passed to other matters, less weighty, such as true love, taxes, and who else might be invited to take up the outstanding share in the summer rent. Roger excused himself for a walk. While the others were clearing the table, a chestnut-haired Viking in jeans and a leather vest appeared at the door.

"Hi. Is Roger Ryder around?"

"No," said Paul. "But I am."

"Roger went for a walk," said Albert. "He'll be back any minute. Would you like to wait for him?"

"No, thanks. Just tell him I was here, okay?"

Albert's mouth had opened and Paul was hugging himself. Franklin coughed.

"What . . . name . . . should we give?"

The Viking treated them to a lovely laugh. "Describe me."

"Did you see that?" said Albert in a stage whisper as the footsteps died down the walk.

"Do you suppose he's in the same house as the tea man?" asked Franklin.

Paul sank into the sofa in a daze. "I'd wear a leather vest, only I catch cold so easily."

"Does a laugh like that get born with you?" Franklin wondered. "Or do you have to practice it?"

"This," Albert swore, "is going to be an arresting summer."

The Viking thought so, too. He raced down to the beach and danced in the darkness, his arms beating salutes in the air. Throwing off his clothes, he dove into the ocean where the moon gloated and swam like a champion. It's so easy! So incredibly easy! No doubts, no mistakes, no waste! A no-fault existence! We speak our own language!

He raced the wet sand like those crazy runners; so easy. Tomorrow, he'd give them a beach parade to set legend, then tea again . . . maybe something in a rough punk this time, with stupid eyes, the kind who dance as if their stomach were a snake.

Cresting the stairs, he paused, his upper back shivering in the cool night, and he spoke his own language. "All you have to be," Roger Ryder said aloud, gravely and slowly, as if promising to take good advice, "is terminally beautiful."

The soap interview was a breeze, but what wasn't, now? For an hour or two, Roger stood at a crossroads: should he show up in one of his new "modes," as he called them, or in the form that matched his professional track record, résumé photographs, and appearances in Madame Podyelka's acting class? The modes, he had noticed, effortlessly won; the old Roger had had to fight for everything. But perhaps a separation of parts was not a bad idea; perhaps looks belonged to romance and talent belonged to acting. Pretty-boy roles were boring, anyway; they seldom led to anything but your total replacement two years later by the next pretty boy. This soap was unreasonably loaded with beauties as it was; two had been written out in the last three weeks. Roger decided to go as a character: as Roger Ryder.

They liked him. They liked his walk, his hair, his bluntness, his watchband. They liked his self-confidence, one of his best acts, always. They asked him where he had been hiding, and he laughed because the night before he had been hiding in the mode of a simian wrestler who dazzled a jaded veteran of Sheridan Square with his dangerous thighs, his unexpectedly shy recollections of life in the ring, and his mastery of the spanking arts.

They asked him why he had laughed, and Roger said, "Well, I'd say it doesn't feel like hiding. On the contrary, it's a rare chance to validate your feelings."

What is? they asked him.

"Acting is," he said.

They brought in an official to meet him and had him read. They told him to try one longish speech as if he were wildly in love with the woman he was addressing, a second time as if he hated her, a third time as if she were his dying mother. Then they took the script from him and asked him to play it from memory, because television is tempo, tempo, and the halt are left behind.

He won; and again he was thinking, It's so easy—before he remembered that this one he had done by himself.

We'll call your agent, they told him, and, you know, it'll go through channels, and like, keep your weekdays free starting June 5, and no, there's no script yet, so come in early and you'll have the morning to get used to it.

No language has words for how an actor feels when he gets a hot job without half trying and work starts in a week and this part can take him *anywhere.* For starters, world history begins to seem trivial in comparison with your future, and your feet get bigger. No, they do!

"You look happy, young fellow."

"You!"

"I knew you'd have good fortune."

They had met near Columbus Circle, minutes after. "You didn't . . ." Roger began. "You can't arrange this, can you?"

"I like my boys well placed," said the gang leader. "Depression clouds the mind. Euphoria clears it. The Norse thought the essential quality in a hero was luck. I like the Norse. Good lines."

"'My wit's diseas'd.'"

"Ah, but you don't lack advancement, that's the important thing. Where will you go tonight? What will you be?"

Roger wondered about that every evening, as he prepared before a full-length mirror behind the bathroom door. He was a Mr. Wizard of the vanity lab, learning by doing. He would experiment with shapes of nose, depths of navel, formats of chest hair. Marvellous how the flesh instantaneously responded to the will; the imagination is quicker than the eye. But when you're already in the topmost class, what sets you

168

apart from the others such—what's 101 percent? A really slick haircut? Roger fleetingly played with innocuous yet arresting flaws—scars, a mole, wild eyes, a limp. Maybe a cane?

What will you be? he wondered again two nights after the soap interview, in the apartment of an old Village avatar, a king of the leather scene in the early Stonewall years and nostalgically resonant even in semi-ruin. Roger, a busty buckaroo, had taken particular care with his face that night, molding till he had something truly shattering. The old leather king very nearly shook his head in disbelief as they traded stares in front of Clyde's.

"I can't decide," he told Roger, "if it's the eyes or the mouth."

"It's both."

Two blocks away, in the tiny studio that had played host to uncountable young princes, Roger saw how raptly one obeys the command of attraction, what concentration lies in the borrowing of beauty. "As you open my pants like a burglar," the leather man breathed, and "I have no choice, as you lead me by the ass to the bed, to get me all set, to ream my ass out for me whether I'm willing or not." Captions to pictures Roger had never seen. "I know what it is, man," the leather man said as Roger laid him down. "You like to see some big stud throwing his rod as you stretch him out, huh? Big, fuckable stud, big dude, to give you what he has. Is that it? Tell me about it. Tell me what you're going to do."

Why should I? Roger thought. You're doing fine all by yourself.

"You make me so hot," the man went on. "And you know it. You're gonna go ahead with it. Yeah, you don't care. Like some guy I met once, this trucker, this big hot dude. Jesus, he was tough." Roger tried to shut him up with some mouth-to-mouth, but he talked right on through. "Oh yeah, romance me. It's so nice. So nice it hurts. So this big dude tells me he knows this guy who makes porn movies and maybe he should audition me. Yeah. So I said I don't know about that stuff, man, and he says, Just come here so I can loosen you up. . . ." Roger stroked the man's thighs as he eased in and at last the man was silent, except, just before he came, when he whispered, "Oh, you are so damn what," which is a somewhat notable thing to have said. And no sooner were they disencumbered than the man more or less threw Roger out.

"I couldn't live up to that, man," the old king told him when Roger asked him to lunch the next day. "I mean, I have my good days, but . . . hell . . ." He looked at the wall, at nothing, faded squares where once hung nude photographs of an achingly beautiful man, this man. He laughed ironically, to please himself. "It's both."

Amiably donning his Stetson, Roger said, "Are you saying you didn't enjoy that?"

"No. I'm saying you didn't."

What will you be? Lose the cowboy, Roger warned himself. It's too hot for that clothing, anyway. I'll be contemporary, loose. No more mercy fucks for old-timers. Let's try some California-style kids, sheer looks and no complications. Three nights later, in the mode of a preppy football hero, Roger picked up a boy hovering near the garage of an office tower. Roger had seen him there before, whistling at women with his co-workers in the garage and setting the pace for the lunchtime stroll. Straights yield to beauty just as gays do, working-class straights especially, because they don't know how to behave around women who aren't their mothers. Instead, they court men.

This boy told his pals that Roger was a cousin and ambled up to him as if a motor were humming in his mid-quarters. The cheek, Roger thought. The cocky lack of cover dodges. That's what they're like; confidence turns them reckless. And their pals will look away and change the subject. His pals did. Everybody spoils them.

It took a long time to land the boy; they like to be persuaded in code. On the way to Roger's, they paused at a sidewalk fruit stand and the boy coolly palmed an apple while the proprietor was helping a fastidious business wimp collect a ripe banana. What did he save, fifty cents?

Roger cursed himself for caring. He tried to think of the boy's callous devilry as showmanship. The boy chomped on his booty as they walked, mouthing out "Like, man" and "Yeah, like" as if they were basic punctuation. He undressed like a peep show come unsprung, giggling and posing. Roger fucked him savagely, to avenge the stolen apple. The boy got mad and shoved Roger off him, so Roger grabbed him by the hair and bounced him off the walls. He was mad, too, it appears.

The boy cursed Roger as he dressed. He kept saying "Fucking crazy, man," and finally Roger grabbed the boy and his clothes and threw them all into the hall. The boy had to snatch the bannister to keep from flying downstairs.

"'Don't know m'own strenth,'" said Roger, in Bullwinkle's voice. You never know what you'll be.

Some actors see life as fun and work as terror, but Roger viewed acting as relaxation. If you're well cast and you know your lines and your public is with you, what else should it be? For the first few days in soap, his part consisted of showing up in General City, embracing about thirty-five relations in law and flesh, befriending twenty men, coming on to twenty women, and, at fadeouts, looking enigmatically menacing. Anyone could play it. But the first mail was good, and being recognized in D'Agostino's by appallingly delighted housewives of both sexes amused Roger. He admired the speed with which the whole thing moved, from "story lag" (the time between script composition and public airing) to "set time" (the taping). Once, they told him, their second biggest male sweetheart was written, taped, and presented dying in a hit-and-run automobile accident, all in four days.

Everyone should live this fast, Roger exulted, stretched out on the couch as he answered his housemates' daydreaming questions about the sudden rash of devastating strangers in the Pines. Sometimes he claimed intimate connection to well-sourced dish; at other times he chuckled when they challenged him. All the questions were, What are they like? Yet everyone thinks he knows what they're like. They speak their own language, converse in the instructive pictorial of bodily parts. To note face, shoulders, hands, is to know what they're like—everyone *thinks*.

How amazing, Roger thought, to know.

One thing he could tell about them: they are never shy. By the time they're seventeen or so even the dullest of them has noticed the interest he excites in others, in the way women show their feelings a little for him, and the way men try to cover theirs. Nice-looking people can be shy, but spectacular people have had it too easy to hold back.

There was a nice-looking fellow at Roger's soap; no one, ever, was shyer. He had virtually grown up on the program, playing someone's child through from early adolescence into young manhood. Roger's character was intricately and repeatedly related to his, yet thus far they had met only in the green room during breaks. His name was Roger, too, yielding a dozen nervous-actor jokes and breaking the ice for them.

"Sometimes I think it's safer to play the sidekick parts," the boy told Roger. "I've seen hot shots here today and . . . you know? But look at me. Twelve years of steady work. And I don't have to do anything. What else could I do, anyway? I never had . . . an ambition. I do what I'm told and I collect my check."

"You don't get much to play with, though, do you?"

The boy shrugged. "I'm not an actor. My dad was in TV then, so they cast me. And I'm easy to use, so I'm still here." He put down his sandwich and shook his head happily. "Believe me, plenty were who aren't."

He had a nice way of shaking his head—a nice head to begin with. He saw Roger watching him and looked away. "Maybe I shouldn't tell you this."

"Why the hell not?"

"Well, you . . . you never know how people will react."

True. Investigate a brazen Puerto Rican in a black muscle shirt and he'd turn out to be soulfully in need of cuddling; a taciturn bruiser might sniffle at an ambiguous comment; a dizzy kid would sacramentally produce rope from under the bed, his eyes on ice. You never know what they'll be.

Now, in Madame Podyelka's acting class, you knew what your fellow actors wanted to be just by what they did with their hands when they began a scene. You knew how the others would react, too. The performer's friends would offer praise tempered by quibble; everyone else would rip the scene to shreds.

"Children, it is life," Madame Podyelka would cry. "It is truth. Outside, it is false. Mistakes. Undirected."

"Do you think acting class would help me?" Little Roger asked Roger Ryder the day he blew a line three times in a row.

"Want to sit in on one? Madame loves guests. She thinks once anyone comes to an acting class, he's bound to come back for more."

"Where is it?"

"In her living room."

Little Roger shrugged in amazement.

"Madame thinks stages inhibit actors. She emphasizes acting in the round."

"I've never acted before an audience," said Little Roger. "I've never even auditioned. I was almost born on TV. Why don't you take me dancing instead?"

"Want to go to the Royal Party?"

The boy tried, failing, to look comically sly. "Does Erika Kane need a tongue-lashing?"

"You know, she's very sweet offstage."

Madame says, "Darlings, there is no offstage. There is not thinking. There are empty performance. Now, let's all practice our anxiety cough. *Odin. Dva . . .*"

Roger had gone out in the mode of a Colt model, more or less, picked up a real one, and had a jazzy time till the next morning, when the model went into a harangue about the infiltration of the American porn industry by extraterrestrials.

173

He gave Roger the ticket to the Royal Party. "They want the best," he told Roger. "Bring your hottest friend."

Everyone was there, they say, but they always say that: to those who weren't. There had been confusion as to how the title related to costume, so some came dressed as royalty while others simply behaved as such. A few discovered intriguing new places in which to wear crowns, and there was an unusual emphasis on drag. But otherwise the Royal was like all Great Parties, a place where one came to worship beauty and to dance—sometimes, but not usually, the same thing. It depends on who is dancing.

The two Rogers did some, but for much of the time they lurked among the sleek clutter. Here and there they grinned at each other. Once, in the excitement, Little Roger put his hand on Roger Ryder's shoulder, almost in passing; sure homage from such a bashful fellow. Paul and Albert came up to rave for a bit. At one point Albert gazed upon Little Roger, then nodded slyly at Roger Ryder.

"Oh! 'I Need a Hero'!" cried Paul, as the music swept in. "I have to! I have to!" He grabbed Albert and they rushed onto the floor.

"Do they think we're lovers?" Little Roger asked. He had seen Albert's signal of approval.

"They think we're dating. They'd think Nixon and Mondale were dating if they walked into a room together. Albert and Paul are romantics."

The boy pocketed his hands, released them, pocketed them. "Are we dating?"

Franklin wandered by. "I hear we have a new housemate."

"Anyone I know?" Roger asked.

"Silly boy," said Franklin, wandering off. "Albert told me *everything*."

Roger hugged Little Roger. "Want to dance?"

Later, waiting for Little Roger to return from the men's room, Roger heard a familiar voice over his shoulder: "The whole gang is disappointed in you."

Roger turned.

"The party of the year, and you come as yourself with a bus-and-truck Heidi."

"He's a nice kid."

"He's dreary as three Kansas picnics."

"I've been all over town, right? in a hundred snappy disguises. Don't I get a night off?"

"Not this night. Here's Georgie. Georgie ought to dance with you."

Georgie, in T-shirt and jeans, looked like the man in whose honor clonestyle was developed. His name was tattooed on his right biceps.

"I don't like beards," said Roger.

Georgie's beard vanished.

"Georgie," the leader warned, "no showboating."

Georgie took Roger by the arm. "Let's find a quiet corner," he said, "and get you nice and ready."

"Wait a minute, I have to—"

"Make it tasty, boys," said the leader.

There was no evading Georgie, Roger sensed; he'd get it over with and find Little Roger in good time. Way off at the edge of the party they found an angle shrouded in darkness. Georgie stood point, his huge back and long arms covering Roger as he flashed into mode as a surfer, dressed to match Georgie.

"Yeah, give me lots of package," said Georgie, feeling Roger's crotch.

"Let's do this thing."

Roger was so used to shifting look that he seldom bothered to view his changes anymore; he saw enough in the eyes of his witnesses. They followed Georgie and Roger as they eased onto the dance floor, reoriented themselves to observe Georgie and Roger, were heard to sing when Georgie wheeled behind Roger to simulate a humping motion.

"Let's take our shirts off together," Georgie whispered, his cheek smoothing Roger's hair. "Do it real slow, where you pull up from the waist with your hands crossed."

Who made him the director? Roger thought; but he did it, because once he had stood at the edge of this scene, wondering what doing it felt like. Smirking at each other like Krakens at a wake, Roger and Georgie parked their shirts in their pants; Georgie moved close to Roger and unfastened the top of his pants. "Yeah," said Georgie. "Now you. Me."

"I don't do windows," Roger replied.

He was about to leave the floor when the clacking of castanets caught his ear and two spectacular men joined them, similarly undressed, one—on the lean but lavish side—playing the instruments and the other—titanic—carrying an assortment of metal equipment on his belt. Each of the newcomers also bore a tattoo on his arm, like Georgie's, "Tony" and "Keeper." Grinning at Roger, Keeper, the metal man, flipped the top of Georgie's jeans open and ever so slightly nodded his head. Georgie reached for Roger and bought his lips with his own. Roger began to struggle almost at once, but Georgie held him so fast he couldn't even shift position, much less get away. Keeper sidled around, pinned Roger's arms behind him, and handcuffed him. Roger sensed every eye in the room on him as the other three men began to stir, sensed that he had been plugged into the vertigo of a million hungry men. Doing it is an elite fantasy for the conqueror; being done to, however, might be all-encompassing. Those who most fiercely resist it pay its fiercest homage.

"New boy, come," Georgie urged. "The handcuff dance."

Tony played his castanets so sweetly that Roger was mesmerized, as by a caress. In another life, somewhere, he heard clapping, music, dishing, shouting, and Keeper telling Georgie, "Make him happen." Swallowing his panic, Roger forced up a smile and slowly shook his head. "Take the cutlery off," he said pleasantly, "or I'll change into a hippopotamus in front of a thousand curious bystanders."

"It doesn't make animals," said Georgie.

"Arnold Stang, then."

"You're no fun," said Georgie, shooting an angry wink at Keeper. Roger was freed. Marching into the crowd to find

Little Roger, he met a rota of stares, as searching as Diogenes. Why was it so easy to smile? Some of them were loving couples, cheating. Roger could not bear a cheat.

He found Little Roger sitting on bleachers near the refreshment table, looking like E. M. Forster when he realized that he might have sailors but would never be a sailor. Better: when he realized that, hell, he wasn't even going to have sailors.

"Hey," Roger said, tapping him on the shoulder. "I have a message for you from Roger Ryder."

"How did . . . I mean, what message?"

"He told me to tell you that he's networking with some advertising people. Stay put and he'll be with you in a few minutes. Okay?"

Little Roger stretched his legs and smiled. "I'll be here."

"One more thing."

"Yes?"

"He says he likes you."

Roger ruffled Little Roger's hair and sped away to meet the gang leader; trouble is never hard to find in an elite gay festival.

"And what," Roger began, "was that punk vignette supposed to be about?"

The leader made the naughty boy sign at Roger, left index finger scraping right one. "You were rude to the gang. Surely I told you how much we count on loyalty."

"Call your hunks off me. I'll make their acquaintance in my time and in my way."

"What better way than at a great place of the culture, and thus, in the disorderly conduct that inspires a million dreams?" He looked almost reverant. "You belong with your kind. You mustn't squander the elegy on wallflowers. You are to be our great invention."

"If you think I'm going to spend time with brainless disco freaks . . . You said they were sharp. And what's all this with the tattoos, may I ask? May I?"

"You'll have one." The leader traced a line of sweat

down the center of Roger's chest. "When your three months are up. Yes, young fellow. You'll take a look of choice, and your new name, and a whole catalogue of chores. Beauty is never boring—and you will party."

Roger calmed down, even laughed. "I still don't believe any of this." He reached behind for his T-shirt. His back pocket was empty.

"You don't believe? In the borrowed eureka of a Galahad? Don't bother; I disposed of your shirt. I hate over-dressing."

"Why don't you use your magic to build up my career?"

"I intend to, when you take the pledge. I fancy we'll call you Gordian, because you make everything so complex. But there is a central cord of inspiring simplicity: you need to suc-ceed."

"That's true of anyone."

"At what, hey? Georgie only wants to dance and sleep. Keeper's great truth lies in the singing of lullabies to runaway orphans."

Roger surveyed the men promenading past them, look-ing, not looking; bright, drugged; dateless, booked. "And Tony?"

"The band's musician. An offbeat fellow. I support al-most any kind of debauchery, but Tony is so heavy that when you speak of a conservative scene he assumes you mean the guillotine is hand-worked instead of electrical. Picturesque. And not without contacts. He was with James Dean at the end. Messy; that was before Jocko joined us."

"Who is Jocko anyway?"

"Jocko is the most irresistible man in the world. Our safety. The exterminator."

Roger looked at the leader, long and hard.

"We have to enforce discipline, no? Be sensible. Don't make me angry. Be useful. Actors can be so influential."

"Look, it's not . . . I don't get what I want out of it."

"You get what there is."

"It was fun at first, but they started stealing fruit and—"

178

"All men are alike."

"—babbling about aliens—"

"All men are whores."

"—and—"

The leader took Roger by the shoulders and bore down on him. "Trivia," he growled. "Performance is the factor! *See?*" He dropped Roger onto a bench. "I can't bear to hurt a beautiful man." He sat next to Roger, held his head, stroked his stomach. "Look around. Isn't it heaven?"

"You're beginning to sound like a costume designer."

"Take a sizzling young cocker home and break his heart or something. Do it for the gang."

Roger got up.

"For me?"

Georgie, Keeper, and Tony barred Roger's path, Tony's castanets dourly cackling.

"Let him go."

Roger went.

"I know better ways."

Roger was so eager to get back to Little Roger that he scarcely bothered to hide his transformation. Three men saw him change out of mode, so debilitated by drugs they could scarcely be said to have eyes at all.

"Your friend," said Little Roger. "No, listen. How did he know who I was? In this crowd?"

Roger paused. "I told him what you were like, so he knew what to look for."

"Come on."

"My point exactly: come on."

Madame Podyelka says it is very easy to play five things at once, harder to play to three, hardest to play one. "Intensity, children," she advises, "is never boring."

At Roger Ryder's apartment, Roger played desire and Little Roger played nothing, hardest yet to play of all. At a point, you must face the other eyes, and then how can you give them nothing? You can look away. But the rest of the cast will touch you.

"Would it be hard to believe," said Little Roger, "that this is my first time?"

Madame says there is no debut. "We have been acting since we were born."

"Just tell me what you're going to do," said Little Roger.

Madame says, "We play the roles as we are cast."

"This is nice, so far," said Little Roger.

"We are cast," Madame adds, "as we need to be."

Roger Ryder has sometimes wondered why, throughout history, men have risked ghastly consequences just to get someone into bed. It can't be for love. Is it because spectacular figures promise a density of sexual release not otherwise to be had? Is it for power or to make a wily story?

Maybe it can be love.

When Roger awoke in the middle of the night, he pulled a corner of the blanket over Little Roger's shoulder, and Little Roger, sleeping, patted Roger Ryder's back and said, "Okay, okay"; and the next morning they chattered while Roger Ryder made coffee, then drank it in silence; and when they were dressed and about to go out, Roger said, "Look—" and Little Roger said, "I guess—" and Roger was amused to think that spectacular men can say anything but everybody else has to speak his mind or stutter. These two decided not to say anything, and walked to the studio in happy confusion. On the way, a soccer player with the shoulders of Beowulf and a name tattooed on his arm waved at Roger.

Madame Podyelka may have been a charlatan, but any class that gives the actor a chance to perform is useful, and Madame's living room was filled with a colorfully various crowd. There were the few gifted actors, a natural clique respectfully hated by the second-raters. There were the opportunists, who would not rest till they were banking movie money. There were the non-pros, using the class as therapy for social problems. Most various of all was Madame, her fingers covering her mouth or eyes as she heard a scene, her body at a tilt, as if to look straight upon the art were to see it too well.

"Now, children, who will give us an improv?" Madame would say in her tenderly inarticulate palette of accents, roughly, "Chu fill gef es in em*prof?*" And the chosen one would be directed to the center of the room and excruciated in free-associative skits. Other students were called upon to play adversary roles, always The Father, The Mother, The Lover; and it was notable that, for all her almost brilliantly irrelevant advices, Madame always cast these supporting roles from the ranks of the crack troops. In his first days in the class, Roger Ryder had been about to drop out when Madame called him up, assigned him his prototypal partners with a doleful wave of her hand, and gave him the most provocative experience of his career. "The Father is very wrathful," Madame moaned, "because the boy wants to be an actor and not go to doctor school."

The Father, a compact, somewhat collegiate chap who had taken part in the Marriage Contract Scene from *The Way of the World* the week before, bore down on Roger with the eyes of Moses and the hands of Grendel. It wasn't Roger's story—his parents were lifelong theatre buffs—but it was *someone's,* surely, and the two men fought as if there were agents in the house.

Roger was barely holding even with The Father when Madame wailed, "The Mother lives only to quarrel with The Father. The boy is her weapon!" Was he ever. Two minutes later, when Madame had Roger seek sympathy from The Lover, he found himself shaking in her arms.

Odd how profoundly someone else's story can affect us. Roger scarcely heard Madame's analysis of his performance, or the tense discussion that followed, though a few assaults on his "honesty" pricked his ears. "It *was* honest, darlings." She turned to Roger. "Was it true?"

"It was . . ." Roger hesitated. ". . . fictions."

Behind him somebody snorted.

"It is a story," said Madame, smoothing out her dress. "It is a role. Is it a true story? Or just a pretty story?"

"I thought it was true," said The Father. "I felt it."

"Of course," said Madame. "I know that you feel, even if you are not tall enough for father parts. Next time, you must portray a tubercular heiress' sympathetic physician, from a poor family, and everyone has no neck and tiny eyes. Now, children, let us discuss *commedia dell'arte a soggetto.*"

Roger viewed improvs with a loathing fascination; they shattered one's defenses instructively. On the Circuit, from the Eagle to the Botel, one mastered evasions; improvs taught plain speech. Cramming soap script in the green room before set time, Roger realized that Madame had made him too good for soap; it was her kind of story, all confrontations, but the lines spun circles of themselves, with little hooks on the ends to snap into the next episodes. Roger's character had become enmeshed in an adulterous triangle, the refurbishing of a luncheonette by idealistic kids, and a tangled international espionage scheme. But, as the writers had to keep everything elastic, he had yet to utter the simplest declaration. It was a job, and a good one—but not acting. "'Why this is hire and salary,'" Roger told his housemates at dinner, "'not revenge.'"

"Have you noticed how much sexier Roger is," said Albert, "now that he's made it to TV?"

"Fame is sexy," Little Roger explained.

"I'm not famous yet," Roger said.

He was something comparable: a batch of notorious men. The Viking, the wrestler, the Colt model, and Roger's other modes were seen and seen again, at tea, on the beach, on Christopher Street, in Bloomingdale's, always in the inviolable solitude of self-esteem. He was emphasizing a short-and-slim creation, a teenager with extraordinarily pale skin and black hair. Everything about the youth was tender and subdued except his cock, which was perversely big. The one time Roger wore this mode to the gym, three men followed him from the locker room to the showers, one to glower, one to dote innocently, one to look pleadingly at him. The Father, Roger thought. The Mother, The Lover. Strung out on the opposite wall and knowing no joy. As the other two watched, The Lover crossed to Roger's side of the room two nozzles away, then moved to the shower next to Roger, so close you could smell the snot hardening in his nose. Roger turned his back on him, but The Lover sucked in his breath and ran a finger up the crack of Roger's ass. Roger jumped as if bitten. "Please," The Lover said. "Just let me touch you . . . please." As he knelt, Roger grabbed his towel and fled.

"At last you're playing for the team," the gang leader told him, tying his sneakers one locker over. "The boys will be so thrilled. They still resent your failure to dance for them at the Royal Party. Keeper says we'll have to tattoo the name Trouble on you, because that's all you are. You know, I believe I like you best of all like this. There's something so dangerous in the mating of youth and power. I notice you took that nerd out to the Pines last weekend. Don't, again."

"I don't take orders from you."

"Nay, you will."

"All right. Now, all *right!*" Roger dug in with a look. "So I ups to him," Jimmy Durante used to put it.

The gang leader examined himself in a mirror.

"We have to talk," said Roger.

"Bench press," said the leader, flexing his pecs. "Go for the burn."

"Listen."

"You made a deal. You were told the rules. You will observe them."

"It was a con. You knew I didn't believe you."

"Monty Clift tried that on me. Look what happened to him."

"It hasn't done anything for me."

"You're not using it, young fellow. You're so bright. Keeper and Tony, now, they are totally unreproachable in bed, ruthless kismet. But they lack smarts. I know. You know. They know. We want brains. That was you, my boy.

You were to be our entrepreneur. And look what? An affair with something in underpants from some shopping mall in New Jersey!"

"How about letting me ride my own wishes?"

"On whose magic?"

"No fightin' in da locka room, peoples," said the attendant, not looking up from his magazine.

The leader pulled Roger into the Jacuzzi room. "I dispose of the gift as I see fit!" he cried. "Six weeks of dabbling remain; then you work for me. Need I recall to you that the more you please me today, the lighter will be your chores later?"

"Fuck him! Fuck him now!" The leader and Roger turned to find the three men from the shower watching them. "That's what he wants!" The Lover spoke.

"No, it isn't," said Roger.

The Lover pushed forward furiously; the leader grabbed him by the hair, swung him around, and threw him against the wall. "Make him know!" The Lover screamed from the floor, as the other two discreetly dispersed. "Doesn't he deserve to know?" The Lover leaped up at Roger, and the leader downed him again with a kick to the stomach.

"Know what?" Roger asked.

The Lover keeled over, holding his belly and dry-heaving.

"Come," the leader told Roger. "Get used to it."

"Know what?"

"Yes; show no pity. I love a heartless man."

"Why should I pity him? He attacked me."

"Come."

The improvs impressed Little Roger, when he came along to Madame's.

Make me know what?

The improvs free you to say what you wouldn't dare say as yourself.

And Little Roger was coming out to the Island, though he could not afford to become an official housemate. He stood on the top deck of the Fire Island Empress and shrugged because some of the passengers were old, and some were unattractive, and some were grouchy. "It's time they knew," Little Roger told Roger Ryder.

"Knew what?"

Little Roger was willing, nay eager, to try an improv. "What makes you think I can't take it?"

"Okay."

"I *can.*"

"Children, what could be meaner?" Madame would say. "But an actor's life is a chain of improvs. No?"

At the soap, they asked him, Could he do a romance with Tina?

"Sure," he replied, though he had a feeling that somewhere deep in the show's plotting he and Tina were blood cousins.

"You haven't gone anywhere in three days," said the leader. "I'm violently peeved."

"Say nothing!" said Madame. "Be *eyes!*"

Yet her improvs were not mimed.

"Darling," she said to Little Roger, "it is now. We will let the friend play The Father, yes? So fitting. So true. And no Mother or Lover. We keep it simple, da? The Father is mad at the boy because he can never do a thing right. The boy is sensitive. The Father is strict. Out of ferocious love, he must teach the boy discipline."

Madame set them in an amusement park. "The boy has an ice-cream cone," Madame intoned. "He must not drop it. *Ferocious love.*"

Fear in his face, Little Roger endeavored to eat his ice cream and earn approval.

"The father loves the boy no matter what he does," Madame groaned.

Roger Ryder played a terse, conflicted father.

"The boy drops the ice cream," Madame mourned.

Roger Ryder slapped Little Roger's face. "Don't cry," he warned, "or I'll slap you again. *Don't you dare cry.*"

Little Roger cried.

Roger Ryder held him. Ferocious love, he thought. The caption.

"No," said Madame. "Yes, but no. It looks so pretty but it is not correct."

"Why was the little boy sad?" asked a student. "Children have the world to play in."

"It was sentimental trash," said another student, an actor who had never had a job in his life except as a masseur. "I feel degraded by your performance here today."

Roger Ryder still held Little Roger.

The leader had trouble finding Roger Ryder alone after that. They met at length early one Friday afternoon as Roger came out of the Pines Pantry with the groceries. "What drivel about an ice-cream cone," the leader reproved. "Real men don't have fathers."

Roger Ryder smiled vaguely.

"Real men kill their fathers, perhaps metaphorically."

Roger walked on.

Keeper loomed up a few yards down the walk in what appeared to be cellophane jodhpurs.

"Hi, Keeper." Roger gave him a minute flash of the Handcuff Man as he passed. "Taking your Hallowe'en early?"

"Yo hey, good buddy." Keeper fell into step with an arm around Roger's shoulders. "Listen, you got to make good with the chief. He gets mad at you, boy, and you are in *bad* news."

"We'll work it out somehow, I guess."

Keeper shook his head. "You don't know him. He goes crazy when he's mad. He's got like . . ." —Keeper searched for the precise term— ". . . these magic powers."

They had stopped at the ferry landing. At the far end of the harbor, a boat was gliding in.

"You got somewhere we could talk, man?" Keeper asked. "For your own good." Roger Ryder dumped his grocery bag on one of the benches facing the water, and sat.

"Talk, Keeper. I'm ears."

"Yeah. Because I just want to help you, see?" Keeper sat. "If you play along, it's a breeze. If you don't play, you lose bad. Now that is the deal. You got no choice. Look, I know you're smart. But I've seen smart guys go up against him before, and they all go down. They *all*. What've you got against us, anyway? We have fun."

The boat disgorged its singles and groups of clones and queens, reveling and grumping, along with the usual persistent straights, largely Mr. and Mrs. Potato Head couples from New Jersey.

"We have fun," Keeper repeated.

Roger looked at him, weighing the risks in honesty. Oddly, Keeper had not chosen to be handsome. It was a rugged face, a good match for the implausibly supreme physique, but not likable. The eyes were nice.

"It's not fun, Keeper."

"You aren't doing it right. Why don't you change into a runaway orphan and come home with me? I'd sure be sweet to you. You wouldn't have to do a thing. I do all the stuff." Keeper was murmuring, drawing Roger close. "Wouldn't that be nice? I love it when a little orphan begs me not to hurt him."

Roger shot him a bad look.

"Now, I never do hurt them. They just think I will because orphans are the most helpless little cuties there ever could be. Don't you see that? Huh? They're so hot when I teach them how to coco."

"Stop. Stop."

"Yeah—"

"Keeper!" Keeper stopped. "It's just not my part, okay?"

Keeper started again. "Do you do the muscleboy who needs a trainer?" He took Roger's hand in his. "One-on-one."

"Keeper, *no*." Roger pulled his hand away, rested it on Keeper's arm.

Keeper shook his head in disapproval.

"Listen, is that arm real or magic?" Roger asked.

"My muscles are mostly real. But I had no chin." They watched the last tired travelers shuffle off the boat, a queen led by an avid dachshund and two plops. One of the mainland teenagers who work the ferry line was rehitching the tyings as they passed, the queen pouting in mock swoon and the plops staring as if eyes were wishes.

"It's funny," Keeper went on. "We don't really look different now from before. You go wild during the first three months and then you settle down into something like you were. Just improved. Except Jocko—he's always changing around somehow. You should stay away from him, man. That dude is radical."

"Keeper, has anyone gotten free?"

"To what?"

"Free of the gang."

"That's what I'm trying to tell you. *No way.*"

"He tricked me. I thought it was some kind of joke—"

"You *used* it, man! He gave you what he promised and you took it. Now you're on the slate, you got to chalk up. Want to sit in my lap and I'll rub your neck?"

"In the dead center of the Pines on a Friday afternoon?"

"So somewhere else."

Roger laughed. "Tell me, do you catch as well as pitch?"

"I pitch to guys who are smaller and I catch from guys who are bigger. Except so far no one is."

Roger looked out at the bay and bit a thumbnail. "Keeper, is this all on the level?"

"You know what side I'm on, man. But what I'm telling, I'm telling straight."

"You want to shake hands? Man-to-man, solemn and honorable?"

"Hey," said Keeper as they shook.

Roger rose. "I like the way your eyes crinkle, Keeper."

"Come here," growled Keeper, throwing his arms around Roger. They held each other for a long time; when they broke, two handsome men on the top deck of the ferry cheered. Roger blushed. Keeper looked on as if he'd never seen a blush before. He felt Roger's cheek and said, "You're a softie, man. You'll never make it. You'll have to give in. Let's go."

Roger retrieved the groceries. "'It would cost you a groaning,'" he replied, "'to take off mine edge.'"

"Ah yes, the Mousetrap Scene. Have you played Hamlet, then?"

Roger blinked at him.

"Besides having no chin," Keeper explained, "I taught English at CCNY. And, now that the jig's up, take a note of caution: 'The play's the thing.'"

"'I'll mark the play.'" More sobered than diverted, Roger left.

"And?" asked the leader, joining Keeper on the bench.

Keeper shook his head. "He will not give."

"The harder the conquest, the surer the surrender."

"He thinks," said Keeper, biting off the words, "that he has something better."

"Gently so."

"Under that bon vivant facade is a smug little snob."

The ferry slowly backed up, veered 120 degrees to starboard, and chugged northward toward the bay.

"When he's done," said Keeper, "I want him. No limits. Okay?"

"Yes, sweet Keeper."

Even if he hadn't seen the look of confusion on Little Roger's face, Roger would have known that something was wrong; one needs a second or two to adjust to the added weight, to the different balance, to being who you are. Yet not till he set the groceries down did he realize who he wasn't: the Viking had suddenly materialized, in running shorts and a cowboy hat. He put the hat on the counter next to the groceries.

Little Roger sat there.

"Roger asked me to drop by," said the Viking.

"He's . . . networking?"

"Not any more."

It is hardest to play one thing. *Odin. Dva.* . . .

Little Roger got up. "Where is he? Now."

The Viking shrugged.

"Are you staying here?" Little Roger asked. "Do you want something?"

The Viking smiled.

"The others will be here soon."

The Viking said, "You look nice."

"We haven't met, have we?"

"We are meeting."

The Viking moved first, but Little Roger stepped forward, too. He smoothed the Viking's arms and sides as they kissed. There is no offstage. The Viking pulled down the boy's swimsuit and heated him up party-style. Little Roger dug his hands into the Viking's shorts and edged them down to his knees. The Viking stepped out of them, murmuring, "Yeah," as he fondled the boy. "Yeah," he urged. "Yeah?"

"Yeah," said Little Roger.

We play the roles as we are cast.

The Viking lifted the boy in his arms and carried him into Roger Ryder's room. He knew where everything was, every prop and feeling; and the one thing that he played was treachery. His own, and others'. A great many others'. So it was not one thing. It was a rich act. Roger noticed, as he expected to, that the boy responded to the Viking with unaccustomed enthusiasm, all shyness put by. Whoever thought he was innocent? And whose improv was it? The leader's.

Roger lay with the boy for a bit after he had had him, stroking his flanks as he purred on his stomach, his legs spread and his toes twitching for more. "What do you want me to tell Roger?" the Viking asked him.

The boy froze for a moment, then went limp again. "Don't tell him anything."

"If he asks, what then?"

"Lie."

"Not for you."

The Viking showered, donned his shorts, and stood in the doorway. Little Roger flipped over onto his back and kicked his legs together in the air. He seemed utterly content. "Where is your house?" he asked.

The Viking said nothing.

"Will I see you again?"

"No."

The Viking left the cowboy hat on the counter.

Roger Ryder found the leader sitting on the bench where Keeper had been. "Now what?" Roger asked him, sitting down.

The leader patted Roger's knee. "It hasn't worked out, has it?"

"Are you going to let me off?"

"Keeper yearns to date you. Will it be tonight?"

"Listen."

"Bad news at your soap, though. I hear you'll be dropped from the saga presently. 'Indefinite leave,' they call it. How did your little friend like the Viking?"

"So you did that."

"I gave you the outfit, no more. What was done, you did. You look so sad. Will you weep?"

Roger shook his head.

"Lucky, with all the boats pulling in. We wouldn't want to be the subject of satirical remarks. Do you surrender? At last, young fellow? Your time's nearly up, anyway."

Roger shook his head.

The leader tenderly scratched Roger's hair. "What am I going to do with you?"

Roger looked at the leader for a long moment. "How can you do this?" he said at last.

"You mustn't be manfully pathetic. Anything but that— one look and I crumble." The leader laughed his nasty noise. "I've taken everything from you. You have no work and no love. What more must I do, tear down your apartment building and revoke your plastic?"

"You cheated me."

"You cheated me, young fellow."

"I won't work for you. I'd rather die."

"Your mind is locked on this point?"

"Yes."

"Nothing will sway you? No consideration of fame or beauty?"

"Worthless."

"Is it now?" The leader sighed profoundly. "Keeper will be so irritated. I expect I'll have to send Georgie to the bus station to find another runaway orphan for him. But so be it. You're too sensitive for our kind of fun. Go. Take another of your reflective walks along the beach. No doubt the whole thing will pass like a mad fancy."

Roger stared at the leader. "Are you . . . letting me off?"

"Let's say that I'm dismissing you. Now go."

Roger ran till he reached the edge of the sea, to wade into it, splashing like a dope and feeling himself emotionally for the sense of reprieve. No one had taken anything from him, in fact; he was back where he had started, a mere summer older with plenty to do. He walked west, watching the sun burn red and the clouds catch it till the sky streaked fire. He would continue to worry more than he hoped, but that was true of most of the people he knew. The ones with great apartments were bored; the ones with great jobs were lonely; the ones with great lovers were penniless. No one has everything. If you could take true satisfaction in any one thing of your choice, what should it be?

Curious shapes drew Roger up away from the water to an amazing monster of a sand castle, a city of tunnels and turrets. Roger looked in wonder. How was such a thing sculpted? With molds and dainty instruments, perhaps, from some antique seaside toy box? It was Eldorado, Xanadu. Who had put in so much time on such a doomed project?

Away up on a patio someone was waving. Roger looked

192

around; he was alone. He waved back, and the figure signaled him to come over.

I don't know anyone in this part of the beach, Roger thought. As he drew near, he saw a man in cut-off jeans, a hooded sweatshirt, and dark glasses.

"I saw you looking at the castle," the stranger told Roger. "It's like a dream. Come close. Yes. Look." The stranger aimed Roger at the sea. "The water overpowers the dream city, and it sinks down, and is obliterated."

"Who built it, do you know?"

"Your smile is trembling." The stranger pulled off his sweatshirt, and Roger caught a glimpse of the man's tattoo as he reached for him. Roger struggled as the first wave swept upon the castle.

"Not yet," Roger cried.

"You won't feel a thing," said Jocko.